WILD HERO

TYSON WILD BOOK SEVENTY ONE

TRIPP ELLIS

D1522419

TRIPP ELLIS

1

_____

"What do you think?" a gorgeous brunette asked with an optimistic grin.

I measured my response but couldn't help but speak my mind. "I think it's a brushstroke on canvas. And I think the asking price is a little too high. But that's me. I'm no expert."

By the crinkled expression on her face, I figured she didn't like my response. "It's much more than just a brushstroke on canvas."

JD and I were in one of those snooty art galleries full of modern art and sculptures of dubious merit. The kind of art that made you scratch your head and wonder. It was hard to see some of these works as anything more than a money laundering scheme. But that wasn't why JD and I were here.

The stunning vixen continued, "It's a statement."

I gave her a curious look. "A statement?"

"A declaration and a question at the same time."

"What's the question?"

"You're asking it right now," she said with a slightly sassy lift of her eyebrow.

She had nice eyebrows. She had nice eyes. She had nice everything. Her tight pantsuit looked professional but offered tantalizing glimpses of the true beauty contained within.

We were playing a game now. I didn't mind it so much.

"What is the nature of art?" she said in a slightly lofty tone.

"Does this really qualify?" I muttered. "Anybody can do it."

"And that's the statement. A democratization of art. Accessibility. Anyone can express themselves, make their own personal statement, and show it to the world."

"And the world can respond in whatever way they see fit."

"True."

"Well, no offense, but I'm not paying that price to hang a brushstroke on my wall. But I'm sure the artist will make a killing."

She smiled again. "We shall see. I'd invite you to our upcoming show, but since you've already expressed disinterest…"

"We like a good party as much as the next guy," JD said, trying to salvage this train wreck.

She considered it for a moment. "Then I'll get you an invitation. What brings you into the gallery today?"

I flashed my shiny gold badge. "This is probably a long shot, but I'm wondering if you recognize this artist's work."

I displayed a picture on my phone that I'd taken of some graffiti. The style of artwork had been popping up on local buildings around the island. It was actually good. A combination of stencil and freehand work. Political in nature, making derogatory comments about our current mayor.

I was no fan of the mayor, and let's just say he wasn't a fan of ours.

This wasn't our usual area of investigation, but with the election just around the corner, the mayor put pressure on the sheriff. He wanted the Special Crimes Unit on it.

Needless to say, this wasn't a high priority for me, but in the effort of smoothing out relations, JD and I would at least go through the motions.

Her eyes lit up a little when she looked at the photo.

"You recognize the work?" I asked, going off her expression.

"No. I'm just amused by the content."

"Not a fan of the mayor's?"

She gave a guilty shrug. "I think this town deserves better."

"Indeed," JD said with a grin.

"The work is good, though," I said. "This isn't your standard tagger. A lot of thought and pre-planning went into this. It took skill to execute."

By her expression, she seemed to agree.

"I figured whoever is responsible has an art background. I thought maybe you'd recognize the style."

She frowned. "I'm sorry, I don't. I don't think there's a lot of crossover between street and gallery artists. But this person shows promise. Perhaps if this work were on canvas instead of the side of a building, it might have value." Then she added, "I think there are many that would agree with its message." She paused. "Might want to check with the art schools on the island. Perhaps the college."

"The artist is definitely proud of his or her work," I said. "They've signed each piece."

At the bottom of each work was a copyright symbol, followed by the name *Glyph Mafia*.

"I'll keep my eyes open," the brunette said.

I dug into my pocket and pulled out a card. "Get in touch if you hear anything."

She took it from me and examined the information.

"I'm sorry, I didn't get your name," I said.

"I'm Sasha," she replied, extending her hand.

We made formal introductions.

"I'll get you an invitation if you're still interested."

"Yes, indeed," JD said with a smile.

Sasha darted away to the counter, grabbed a postcard, then sauntered back to us. She handed me the postcard with a smirk on her plump lips.

The promo piece was in black and white with an elegant script. An abstract work of art was the focal piece. At the bottom of the postcard, the date and time of the event were in bold font along with a notice that there would be complementary hors d'oeuvres and cocktails. Who could pass that up? On the back of the promo piece was a picture of the artist, along with the artist's statement.

Did I ever put my foot in my mouth. I looked from the card to the stunning brunette. "You're the artist?"

She smiled.

"I hope I didn't offend you with my commentary," I said.

"I have a thick skin. And the truth is never offensive. Your perception is as valid as anyone else's." Then she added. "I just hope everyone that comes to the event doesn't share your same opinion."

2

"Did your IQ suddenly drop?" JD asked as we stepped outside the gallery. "When a hot girl asks your opinion on a piece of art—hell, when she asks your opinion on anything—you say, 'Hmm, I'm still collecting my impressions. What are your thoughts?' Then you agree with everything she says. Like attracts like. Common ground."

I laughed. I didn't need JD to give me dating advice. Though he did seem to have the magic touch when it came to the ladies.

"Nothing wrong with being confident in your own convictions, even if they are contrary," I said.

He couldn't really argue with that.

We climbed into the convertible Porsche 911 GTS, and Jack cranked up the engine. The flat six rumbled to life, and classic rock blasted through the Bose speakers.

"I think I'm going to do it," Jack said.

"Do what?"

"Run for mayor."

My face wrinkled, and I looked at him like he was crazy. "Have you lost your mind?"

"It's all there, I can assure you."

"Election day is less than two months away. You've got no time to launch a campaign. Have you given this any real thought?"

He frowned at me with a dismissive face.

"What do you know about running city government?"

"A hell of a lot more than that nimrod we've got in office now. And I'm not corrupt."

"Do you know what kind of a time commitment you're talking about? Day in and day out, dealing with bureaucracy and red tape. Fielding complaints from God and everybody. The job is putting out fires nonstop, 24/7. Is that something you're really interested in?"

He gave a halfhearted shrug.

"And you wouldn't be dealing with our best and brightest. People with any sense don't go near that."

"I think I could really make a difference. Somebody's gotta clean up this town."

"I think you and I are doing a pretty good job where we're at."

"Yeah, but I'm talking about real change. It all starts with the top. Shit rolls downhill."

"And what am I going to do? Work Special Crimes alone? You won't have time."

"You'll be my Chief of Staff."

I gave him a flat look.

He shrugged. "What? It's a prestigious position with lots of power."

"I'm not in this for the power and certainly not the money."

Jack frowned at me again.

"Look, I'll support you if this is what you want to do. Just be absolutely certain before you start down that road. Might just get what you wish for."

"Somebody's gotta do something."

"Jim Brooks has got a good chance," I said.

Jack shook his head. "I don't think he's any better, and I'm not sure he can pull it off. Despite everything, our mayor still has a lot of support." He shook his head. "People love to vote against their own interests."

I thought it was a crazy idea, but with such little time between now and Election Day, I didn't really think there was much chance, anyway. I'd let him have his little fantasy. He could play politician for a month, shaking hands and kissing babies, then it would be back to business as usual. I'm sure somewhere in the back of his mind, this was a publicity stunt. More advertising for the band. Another opportunity to get his face in front of the crowd.

Once Jack had gotten the news that Scarlett's biopsy was clear, he was a new man. That heavy cloud hanging over him vanished. The sparkle in his eyes was back, and the optimism about the future had returned. I wasn't about to do anything to dampen that spirit.

The old Jack was back.

The county had recently settled its civil suit with Wendell Carver, who was now a rich man. He made a full recovery, and when Paris interviewed him, he and his wife had glowing things to say about everyone involved, including the mayor. What could have been a potential scandal that would have surely derailed his re-election got swept under the rug. Now, Wendell was the poster boy for the mayor's campaign. Just an everyday guy, shilling for the mayor. But with his new, fat bank account, he wasn't really Joe Average anymore, and he certainly wasn't driving a garbage truck. I heard through the grapevine that his wife filed for divorce after the settlement went through.

Paris still had footage of the mayor soliciting a prostitute, but she was keeping that in her bag of tricks, saving it for a rainy day. I had my suspicions that the footage would come out as an October surprise. Something told me it was time to grab the popcorn and see where this circus went.

The sheriff buzzed my phone.

I answered, "Mayor Donovan's office."

"What!?" he groaned, "Good Lord. He's not really...?"

"What's going on?" I said, changing the subject.

"I need you two imbeciles to get to the warehouse district."

"What happened now?"

3

F irst responders swarmed. Red and blue lights flashed and flickered. An ambulance pulled from the scene just as we arrived.

A body lay amid a pool of blood, surrounded by scattered debris on the loading dock.

JD drove into the warehouse parking lot, which was encircled by a chain-link fence. It had seen better days. There was no gate, and anyone could come or go. The four-story red brick building had stood for over a century. Inside the chain-link fence was a silver four-door sedan parked next to the loading dock. Emergency vehicles filled the area around it.

We weren't far from the practice studio. It was just around the corner.

JD parked the Porsche, and we hopped out and approached the scene.

Brenda hovered over the remains, wearing her pink nitrile gloves. The man had been shredded with blistering shrapnel. Obviously, the victim of a bomb blast. The warehouse door had been blown from its hinges. The victim had apparently triggered the bomb when he attempted to open the door. The blast knocked him several feet back, and he was partially hanging over the ledge of the loading dock. His right arm was a few feet away in the parking lot. Scattered debris speckled the ground, still smoldering.

This was fresh.

The acrid scent of gunpowder still lingered in the air. It was probably a simple pipe bomb. The fragments that littered the area would reveal the truth.

Pipe bombs were relatively easy to make. A pipe and a few end caps from a hardware store, gunpowder packed tight, a fuse, and a battery. If you wanted to be particularly vicious, you could wrap the exterior with ball bearings, nuts, bolts or any type of projectile that would rip through muscle and fascia, making the explosion all the more devastating.

You had to be evil to make one of these things.

And a coward.

With a pipe bomb, you wouldn't be around to see the results of your handiwork. You didn't necessarily have to witness the devastation firsthand. It made it easier for some people to justify in their minds. It wasn't as up close and personal as plunging a knife into someone's belly. You didn't feel the warm blood on your hands. You didn't see the fear of death in your victim's eyes. You didn't smell the tinny metallic scent of blood or their last breath.

That took a different kind of personality.

Sheriff Daniels looked on with a grim face.

It wasn't long before a black SUV with tinted windows pulled into the lot. Out hopped two men in suits, wearing dark aviator sunglasses. They had *federal agents* stamped across their foreheads. Something told me there was more to this scene than first met the eye.

"What's going on?" I muttered to the sheriff.

"Your guess is as good as mine. But something tells me we're about to find out," he said, noting the incoming federal agents.

"I'm Special Agent Dalton, and this is my partner, Special Agent Nash," a man in his 30s said as he reached us.

The two had trimmed brown hair, cut tight on the sides. Dalton was a little taller than Nash.

"I take it the victim is one of yours," Daniels said.

Dalton nodded after a grim glance at the body on the dock. "Special Agent Luke Bishop. He and his partner were working undercover."

"What type of undercover work?" I asked. "Counterfeiting?"

Dalton nodded. "They've been trying to bring down Viktor Nevsky. Russian cartel member. Suspected of moving counterfeit dollars overseas, laundering them through Third World countries with less stringent monitoring, funding terror cells, drug trafficking, you name it. We've gotten close a number of times, but he's always been one step ahead. Agents Bishop and Foster were supposed to meet him here today. Clearly, it was a setup." He paused and glanced around. "Where is Agent Foster?"

"She's been taken to the hospital," Daniels said.

Dalton gave him a look, begging for more information.

"I'm not sure of her condition."

A solemn frown tensed his face. "Not to step on any toes, but we'll be taking over this investigation. Of course, we welcome all the assistance we can get. We'd like to establish a joint task force. I don't have to tell you how badly we want to bring Viktor Nevsky down."

"We'll do everything we can to facilitate your investigation," the sheriff said.

We exchanged information with the two Secret Service agents. They moved toward the remains as Brenda continued to evaluate the scene.

It wasn't long before the ATF and the FBI arrived. Paris Delaney and her news crew weren't far behind. I knew the ambitious blonde wouldn't miss this. It would be a top story.

The sheriff muttered to me, "This may be their investigation, but this is still my county. I want you two to get over to the hospital and talk to Agent Foster, if she's still able to speak. Find out everything you can about this Viktor Nevsky."

"We're on it," I said.

4

The waiting room of the ER was packed. If you weren't dying, it would be a long wait. Sniffles, sneezes, and coughs filled the air. A construction worker wearing a flannel shirt clutched his bloody hand. An old man hunched over with a nasal cannula and a tank of oxygen sat next to him. The pale overhead fluorescents made everyone look like they'd barely survived the zombie apocalypse. There were scuffs and scrapes, broken bones, and high fevers. Kids played with toys on a small table in the corner.

Paris Delaney appeared on the flatscreen mounted on the wall. She continued to report live from the warehouse. "Earlier today, an explosion took the life of one man and wounded a woman who is now in critical care. Details are limited at this time, but we will keep you up-to-date as the story develops. As you can see behind me, investigators are combing through the fragments of what they believe to be a bomb." She rambled on a bit more, then finished her segment with, "I'm Paris Delaney, and you heard it from me first."

I thought it was odd that Agents Dalton and Nash hadn't made an appearance at the ER yet, but maybe they knew something I didn't.

Agent Foster had been triaged and taken straight back. I didn't know what condition she was in, and the receptionist at the front desk wouldn't divulge any information. Sometimes, they were cooperative. Sometimes, they weren't. Depended on who you spoke to.

It wasn't long before Dr. Parker burst through the double doors and waved us back. He wore teal scrubs, a surgical cap, and a mask.

JD and I sprang to our feet and hustled across the waiting room to join him.

"She's okay," Parker said. "A few minor scrapes and burns, but nothing major. I pulled a piece of shrapnel from her thigh. All in all, she got lucky."

He escorted us through the maze of seafoam green hallways to a patient room. He stepped inside and introduced us. "Agent Foster, these are Deputies Wild and Donovan. Do you feel like taking visitors?"

She nodded, and Dr. Parker stepped out of the room.

Olivia Foster looked pretty good, considering her situation. Anybody who could retain a vibrant glow after nearly getting incinerated had something special. She was easy on the eyes. Her chocolate hair hung in waves to her shoulders. Her tawny eyes were sharp and focused. She had elegant features and smooth skin. The silly hospital gown obscured her figure, but I'm sure she kept herself in good shape. You didn't see many field agents that had let themselves go.

"How are you feeling?" I asked.

"I'm feeling pissed off. And you?"

"I don't know if you've heard the news about your partner..."

She gave a somber nod.

"I'm sorry."

Her eyes misted. "Bishop was a good agent and a good father. I feel terrible for Lauren and the kids. Has anyone told them yet?"

"I'm not sure."

The monitor beside the bed blipped with vital statistics— heartbeat, oxygen saturation, blood pressure. An IV dripped into her forearm.

"Dr. Parker says you're gonna be okay."

"I'm ready to get out of here."

"I'm sure you are," I said. "If you're up to it, I'd like you to tell me everything you know about Viktor Nevsky."

"This is a federal matter."

"We're just here to provide assistance."

"Nevsky is a scumbag. I don't care what I have to do—he's gonna face justice."

"We'll help you catch him."

"I don't want to catch him," she said. "I want to kill him."

I could relate to her situation. If anything happened to JD, I'd be out for blood.

"What were you doing at the warehouse?"

She sighed. "We'd been working the case for months. Nevsky recently lost one of his major suppliers. We busted the supplier a month ago. We heard Nevsky was in the Keys, working out a deal with a new supplier. We wanted to get in on the action. Bishop and I had gone deep undercover. We managed to get an introduction. He obviously liked our product. We were supposed to meet Nevsky himself at the warehouse and deliver $2 million in what he thought were counterfeit bills. They were tagged with chips embedded in the paper. They were trackable, and we would be able to see the movement of the currency through his network around the globe. It would have been a huge coup. I'm not sure how he caught on. We were careful. Our backgrounds were solid."

"Could there be a mole in your department?" I asked.

She scoffed at the notion. "No. That's ridiculous."

"Is it?"

She considered it for a moment. A frustrated breath escaped her plump lips. "I guess anything is possible. Money talks."

"Maybe you should be careful who you discuss this case with?"

"Maybe I shouldn't discuss it with you."

"Suit yourself," I said.

We stared at each other for a long moment.

"We talked to your colleagues, Dalton and Nash," I continued.

"I did, too. They're still at the scene. I told Dalton I was fine. I expect to be out of here in no time."

"What will you do next?"

"Nevsky is on his yacht here in Coconut Key. I plan on paying him a visit. My cover is already blown."

"Why give him the satisfaction of letting him see you upset?"

"I'm not upset. I'm pissed off. Two very different things."

"We'll talk to him for you," I said.

"Thank you, but this is personal."

"Do you have anything to connect him to this?"

Her lips tightened, and she shook her head.

"Who's this new local supplier?" I asked.

"We don't know."

JD looked at his watch, then nudged me with his elbow. The Fury Fest was tonight, and we needed to get over to Taffy Beach for the soundcheck. It had been a full day already, and the adventure was just beginning.

I dug into my pocket and handed Olivia Foster a card. "Get in touch if you need anything."

Her hypnotic eyes studied the card, unimpressed.

"You sure you don't want us to talk to Viktor?" I asked.

5

A sea of people filled Taffy Beach. The crowd rivaled the best Spring Break had to offer. The stage was massive, with towering speakers, giant flat-panel displays, and a helluva lighting grid.

Banners for Wild Fury whiskey were everywhere.

Paris Delaney was on the scene and interviewed the band backstage. The guys soaked up the limelight.

Iron Tiger opened the evening. They were bringing '80s hair metal back with spandex and neon. The *Royal Peasants* took the stage afterward and dazzled the crowd with their brand of prog-rock. Faye Vicious held together the rhythm section with style. She and Jagger had put aside their differences, and she certainly brought an exciting dynamic to the band.

We huddled backstage in the makeshift green room, preparing for the show. Dizzy ran through scales on his guitar, Styxx tapped out beats on a practice pad, and Crash just chilled with a beer. Jack went through his vocal warmup, and he sounded pretty good. Tonight would be the test.

"This is the first major show since the original lineup is back together," Paris asked. "Are you nervous?"

"Hell no," JD said. "We're tight and better than ever."

"Expectations are high. What if you don't live up to them?"

The band exchanged uncertain glances.

"Are you trying to plant the seeds of doubt?" JD asked, growing annoyed.

"No. Of course not. But it's a real question."

"It's not a real question because Wild Fury doesn't disappoint."

The band hooted and hollered.

"How's your voice?" Paris asked. "You've had trouble lately."

I don't think she was intentionally trying to stir anything up, but she was so used to finding people's pain points and exacerbating them that she couldn't help herself.

"My voice is 100%. Never better."

"What if you can't hit those high notes like you used to?"

Jack's face tensed, but he steadied himself.

"Thrash has been through an extensive voice rehabilitation program," I said, intervening. *Thrash* was Jack's stage name. "I have full confidence in his ability to put on a great show."

I was nice about it, but the look in my eyes and my tone were unmistakable. It was time for her to back off.

"I have no doubt that Wild Fury will give the audience their money's worth," she said.

"And stick around for the end of the show," JD said. "I've got something special planned."

The ambitious blonde lifted a curious eyebrow. "Are you willing to give me a sneak peek?"

"You'll have to wait, just like everyone else." Jack smiled.

Paris finished the interview by looking into the camera and saying her tagline. When the camera finally cut, she said, "I know you guys are going to have an awesome show."

"Damn right we are!" JD said.

"Break a leg."

The Royal Peasants put on a great show, and the crowd ate it up. They came off stage hyped up, drenched in sweat, the mass of revelers roaring. The band flooded into the green room, full of smiles and enthusiasm. There were high-fives and congratulations all around.

"That's the biggest crowd we've ever played for," Jett said. "This was a great idea, Tyson!"

"Something tells me we'll do more of these," I said.

"More acts and stretch it out over several days," Jack added.

The crowd chanted, "Fury! Fury! Fury!"

"I guess we're up," JD said.

The band had a pre-game huddle, and JD said a few simple inspirational words. "Let's go out there and kick ass!"

There were more hoots and hollers, then the guys marched out of the makeshift green room and gathered stage-left. The lights went down, and the intro music played along with an animation on the flat panels.

Cheers of anticipation filled the air.

It was time.

I hustled onstage and took the microphone as a brilliant beam spotlit me. The blinding light squinted my eyes and obscured the crowd. I soaked in the moment for a second as the audience kept cheering and chanting.

Finally, I said the magic words. "Please welcome to the stage... the mighty... Wild Fury!"

The noise from the sea of people was deafening.

Dizzy hit a power chord off-stage, and the grinding sound of his guitar exploded through the massive speakers.

Styxx jogged to the candy-apple red drum set, climbed onto the throne, and stomped out a beat. Crash took the stage, followed by Dizzy.

The crowd went wild when Jack strutted on stage, his fists above his head in triumph. He howled into the microphone, "Helloooo, Coconut Key! Did you miss us?"

The crowd roared.

"We're baaaaack!" he sang.

The band burst into *Phoenix Rising*.

JD belted out the first verse, and the horde of revelers went crazy. There were a few nervous glances among the guys leading up to the chorus. Would Jack be able to hit the high notes? It wasn't just Paris who had her doubts.

It all came down to this moment.

This would define Wild Fury going forward. Either Jack had his voice back, or he didn't. And if the band didn't nail this show, it could derail their comeback.

The chorus came around, and Jack filled his lungs. He howled the lyrics with fury and passion, and his voice remained solid.

He didn't miss a note.

I couldn't help but grin. The Fury was back.

The band kept cranking out hit after hit all night long. They sounded just as good at the end of the show as they did at the beginning. Jack's voice showed no sign of fatigue.

They played three encores, and after the last song, the band gathered at the front of the stage and took a bow to an elated crowd.

They all soaked up the moment. We'd all fought hard to get back to this point. I think Jack almost got a little misty-eyed.

"I just want to say how grateful we all are to be here tonight. And how grateful we are to all of you for sticking with us through thick and thin," JD said.

The crowd howled.

"I promise we are going to rock harder than ever before!"

That was met with resounding approval.

"We've played a lot of places, but nothing beats a hometown audience. I can't tell you how much this city and the people in it mean to me. That's why I've decided to run for mayor. It's about time we had someone in charge who actually cares about this island. And with me in office, you know it's gonna be a good time."

The crowd seemed to like that idea.

"Thank you! Goodnight!" JD said before departing the stage with the band.

"Mayor? Are you serious?" Crash asked as the band plunged down the steps from the stage.

"Somebody's gotta do it."

"Dude, that would be cool. We can get rid of the noise ordinance."

I laughed. "Something tells me that's not a platform to run on."

As a band, we'd run into issues with the noise ordinance here and there. Anything over 50 decibels after 11:00 PM was a ticketable offense. A loud whisper could put you over the limit.

Jack answered plenty of questions, mainly *how would he have time for the band*?

"If anything, I'll have more time for the band," Jack said.

I stifled a scoff.

"It's 9-5," he continued, completely delusional. "Evenings and weekends free."

Nobody bought it.

As the crowd slowly filtered from the beach, the crew started breaking down the stage. It would be an all-night affair to pick up the trash, remove all the vendor tents, and return the beach to its pristine state. Pinky and Floyd broke down the equipment and were in charge of getting it back to the practice studio.

It was a lot of trouble to go to for a one-night event. The next time we did the Fury Fest, I would definitely plan out a multiple-day event and line up dozens of bands. But this was a proof of concept. We pulled it off, and I knew I could coordinate it. Jack had his voice back, and the band was firing on all cylinders.

Life was good.

Of course, the band was swarmed with groupies after the show. We invited a select few back to the *Avventura* for an after-party, where the usual debauchery ensued. We were all on cloud nine.

The sheriff put a damper on things when he called in the morning.

6

"When was the last time you saw Vernon?" I asked a CNA at the Sunset Palms Senior Living facility.

"Yesterday afternoon, just before I got off shift," Mike said. "I stopped in to tell him goodbye."

Mike was a likable guy in his mid-30s. He had short chocolate hair, dark eyes, and a somewhat square face. He was a little doughy around the midsection and under the chin, but generally in good shape. His trimmed mustache and goatee toughened up his look. He wore teal scrubs, and an ID badge was clipped to his chest pocket.

Sunset Palms was the kind of place where you signed over your home and rode out the rest of your days in their care. For that, you got a small room with a kitchenette and a balcony. If you were lucky, you even got a view. The place offered full services, from skilled nursing to assisted living.

Of course, there was a host of recreational activities for the more mobile—billiards, ping-pong, tennis courts, and even pickleball. Social activities were part of the curriculum with regular bingo nights, senior mixers, and dances. There were group outings to the zoo, the museum, the aquarium, and other sites about town. Of course, there were a lot of folks that just sat in the TV lounge in a vegetative state.

The air had that stale smell of mothballs and muscle cream. Classical music filtered through the speakers in the ceiling.

Daniels had told us to get over here and investigate.

"When did Vernon go missing?" I asked.

"According to the records, he was here at bed-check."

"When is that?"

"Usually around 9:00 PM. I checked the logs. Monica made the rounds in his wing."

"Is she here now?"

Mike shook his head. "No, she works the evening shift." Then he added, "I can give you her number."

I nodded. "And you think Vernon wandered off?"

"This wouldn't be the first time he'd taken it upon himself to go on an excursion. It's not a prison. The residents are allowed to come and go as they please. But Vernon is in our cognitive care unit, so they aren't supposed to leave unaccompanied. Still, there's nothing keeping them here."

"Where has he gone when he's run off before?"

"He usually doesn't go far. I found him at the Reef Shack a few times. He likes to go in and have a beer at the bar. That was my first thought when I discovered he was missing. I called down there, but they said they hadn't seen him. We found him at the grocery store once. I called there as well, but they hadn't seen him either. That's when I began to get worried."

"How bad of shape is he in?" I asked.

"He's 95 years old, strong as an ox, and gets around better than most people in this place. He's just a little forgetful. At times, he's sharp as a tack, and other times, he doesn't remember his own family. It's kinda crazy. You can get him talking about the war, and he'll recount events in meticulous detail. Ask him what he had for breakfast, and he might not be able to tell you. I'm sure it's so frustrating for his loved ones."

"Does he have any family on the island?"

"His granddaughter lives here. She comes to visit a lot. I think she's all he has left."

"Has she been notified?"

Mike nodded. "I called her. She said she's on the way. She was in Pineapple Bay. She should be here soon."

"What's her name?" I asked.

"Paige. Really sweet girl. Cute."

"Does she live in Pineapple Bay?"

"I don't think so, but I'm not sure."

"Does Vernon have a cell phone?"

Mike nodded. "Yeah, but it's in his room."

A thin frown tugged my lips. There went the idea of tracking him.

"I'd like to see his room."

"Certainly." Mike led us down the hallway.

We passed by several rooms. Many doors were open, and the sound of televisions filtered into the hallway.

Keys jangled as Mike fumbled through a dozen of them on a keychain. He found the right one, slipped it into the slot, then opened Vernon's door. He pushed inside the foyer, flipped on a light, and held the door for us.

We stepped inside and looked around. The small space resembled a hotel room. There was a bathroom with an oversized door and plenty of stainless steel handles around the toilet and the shower stall. A small kitchenette with a refrigerator, induction stove, microwave, and dishwasher gave residents meal autonomy if they wanted it. Beyond that was a small sitting area and a double bed, followed by another small sitting area and sliding glass doors that led to a patio that was enclosed by a fence. I guess it wasn't a bad place. But the notion of it seemed sad.

The walls were lined with pictures of Vernon and his loved ones. The faded images captured various stages of the man's life. There were several black-and-white photos of Vernon as a 17-year-old in his Navy uniform. There were dozens of photos of him on Navy vessels during the war with his buddies. There was a progression of photos of a beautiful woman who I assumed was Vernon's wife. The photos followed her through the years as she aged. There were pictures of his children and his granddaughter.

"He's a World War II veteran," I observed.

"Oh, man, does he have stories," Mike said, his eyes filling with awe and wonder.

"I bet."

Vernon's phone rested on the nightstand by the bed. I picked it up but was met with the familiar security screen. I would have liked to look at the most recent calls and texts, but Vernon didn't strike me as the type of guy who was continually glued to his phone.

A small flatscreen TV sat atop the dresser, and the shelves were filled with books—paperbacks of old men's adventures.

"Do you think he just walked out of here in the middle of the night?" I asked.

Mike shrugged. "I guess."

"What's security like around here?"

"We usually have an armed security guard on duty, and the CNAs make regular sweeps of the units."

"Do you think he could have been kidnapped?"

Mike's eyes rounded, and he stared at me for a moment. "I guess anything is possible. But why would anyone kidnap Vernon?"

"Does his granddaughter have access to a lot of money?"

"I don't know. There haven't been any ransom demands. At least, not that I know about."

"What kind of relationship does he have with the rest of the staff and other residents?"

Mike thought about it for a moment. "I guess he gets along with everybody. Almost everybody. I mean, he's a really neat guy. What a life he's lived."

"Who are the people that he *almost* gets along with?" I asked.

ell, Vernon's not exactly on the best of terms with Albert," Mike said.

"Who's Albert?" I asked.

"The two used to be friends until Phyllis came along."

"Let me guess. Vernon stole Phyllis from Albert."

"Something like that. Not to gossip, but Phyllis changes her mind like most people change underwear. One week, she's in love with Albert. The next, she's in love with Vernon. Made things pretty contentious between the two."

"I would imagine," I said.

"You don't think...?"

"I think a lot of things," I said. "How capable is Albert?"

"Capable of what? Kidnapping? Murder?" he said in a doubtful voice. He shook his head dismissively. "No way. Albert needs a walker to get around. And anybody trying to kidnap Vernon would have their hands full. The old guy still has a lot of fight in him. He can be ornery at times." Mike paused, "Though the two did almost get into it last night at dinner."

"What do you mean?"

He told me the story. Basically, a couple nonagenarians talking trash.

"Has Vernon expressed a desire to go anywhere recently?" I asked.

"He always joked about breaking out. Says he wants to go on one last adventure. He always said he wanted to climb Everest, but somehow I don't think that's happening. He said he wanted to go to Paris, Venice, see the Swiss Alps. I think he has a lot of bucket list items."

A breathless young woman burst into the room with bright eyes. "I came as soon as I could."

"Paige, this is Deputy Wild and Deputy Donovan. They're with Special Crimes."

"Do you think he's okay?" Paige asked.

She was a striking young woman with golden blonde hair that kissed her shoulders, smooth skin, full lips, and tantalizing green eyes. She was probably about 24 and had a wholesome, innocent vibe about her.

"I'm sure he's fine," I said. "I don't think we need to go into panic mode just yet. I talked to the sheriff. He put out a Silver Alert on Vernon. Can you think of anywhere he might have run off to? A place he might have mentioned recently?"

She thought about it for a moment and shook her head.

"I'll give you guys some privacy so you can talk," Mike said.

I asked him for Monica's number and got his contact info before he left. He excused himself and stepped out of the room.

"When was the last time you talked to your grandfather?" I asked.

"Last night. Just after dinner. We try to talk every day."

"So, you two are close?"

She nodded.

"Did he mention any plans for the evening?"

"No, he said he was going to watch a little TV." She frowned. "Half the time when I call, he doesn't know who I am. Sometimes, he feels like talking. Sometimes he doesn't. That's why I try to call every day and stay fresh in his mind. I come to visit when I can, and he just..." She frowned, and her eyes filled. "It's so hard, you know? One minute he's there. The next minute he's not. One time, he accused me of being an imposter. Wanted to know where his real granddaughter was." Her misty eyes spilled over. "I just want him to look at me and really see me. Tell me he loves me one more time."

"I'm sorry you're going through that."

She wiped away the tears, pulled herself together, and gave an appreciative nod.

"Are you his only family?"

She nodded again. "Both of my parents died in a car accident several years ago."

"My condolences."

"We're all each other has left," she said with a sigh. "It's so hard, you know? There's so much the doctors don't tell you. It's more than just memory that goes. Eventually, his brain will forget how to do basic functions like swallowing and breathing. He's dying this slow, miserable death."

I had such empathy for her situation. It must have been horrible to watch Vernon deteriorate.

"Do you live here in town?"

She nodded. "I was visiting a friend in Pineapple Bay."

"Can you think of anywhere Vernon might have gone?"

"He likes the Reef Shack. We found him one time at the VFW. He made his way to a football game once."

"How do you usually find him?"

"He gets lost, then asks someone for help. Fortunately, there's always been somebody around to clue into the fact that he's not all there," she said, tapping her noggin. "By some miracle, he gets back here. I keep telling them they either need to lock him in or put an ankle bracelet on him. But I can't force that on him, and he doesn't want it. I'm not gonna treat him like a prisoner. I wouldn't want somebody to do that to me."

"We'll do everything we can to see to his safe return."

"I appreciate that."

We exchanged numbers, and I told her to get in touch if she needed anything or heard from Vernon.

"Do you have a current photo of him?" I asked.

Paige nodded. She dug her phone from her purse, scrolled through the photos, and sent the most recent picture to my phone.

We stepped out of Vernon's room and talked to a big guy named Otis in the hallway. He was about 6'3" and built like a lineman. He looked like a mean, imposing figure, but when he spoke, he had a gentle demeanor.

"The last time I remember seeing Vernon was yesterday at lunch," Otis said. He frowned. "I hope he's okay. Hell, I wouldn't be surprised if he found his way to the bus station and is long gone."

"Did he ever express a desire to travel?"

Otis chuckled. "Hell, one time I checked on him, he was all dressed up with his bags packed, ready to go. I asked him where he was going, and he said he was going to his ranch in Montana." Otis paused. "I'm not sure how he planned on getting there. I let him keep talking about it, and eventually, the thought passed. I asked Paige if he had a ranch in Montana, and she said that's where he grew up."

I gave Otis a card, then we talked to a few other staff members who echoed what Mike had said.

We found Albert in his room. The door was slightly ajar, and the sounds of the TV filtered out. I knocked lightly and poked my head into the foyer. "Albert?"

"What do you want?"

I made introductions as we stepped into the foyer and walked into the living area. Albert sat in a recliner, watching a game show. He was a heavyset man in his 90s with a puffy face, white hair parted in the middle, and a mustache that almost curled at the ends.

A silver walker with yellow tennis balls on the feet stood at the ready near the chair.

I flashed my badge for good measure. "We just have a few questions for you."

"Whatever it is, I didn't do it," he said with a mischievous grin.

"It seems Vernon has gone missing. You wouldn't know anything about that, would you?"

His face wrinkled. "Missing? Like how?"

I shrugged. "I'm sure he just wandered off."

"Maybe he fell off a cliff," he said with disdain in his dim eyes.

"There aren't any cliffs around here."

"Well, maybe he drowned."

"That's not nice to say."

Albert frowned at me. "He's not a nice man."

"I heard you two carry a grudge."

He scoffed. "Ha! Ain't no grudge. I hate the son-of-a-bitch."

"Tell us how you really feel," JD muttered.

"I just did."

"I thought you two used to be friends."

"Ha!" he scoffed again. "He doesn't know the meaning of friendship. If he did, he'd keep his hands off my girl."

"Can't Phyllis make up her own mind about who she wants to be with?"

"That's the problem. She can't seem to make up her mind at all. I dated her first. That means it's hands-off. Vernon should have known better."

"When was the last time you saw Vernon?"

He thought about it for a moment. "I reckon it was at dinner last night."

"Did he mention anything to you about escaping?"

"Nope. We don't talk."

"Maybe you guys ought to bury the hatchet."

"I'd like to bury a hatchet in his skull."

"If he turns up with a hatchet in his brain, I'll know where to look."

Albert frowned at me.

"It's my understanding you two had words at dinner last night."

"I'd have punched his lights out if there wouldn't have been someone there to stop me."

"Want to tell me about the altercation?"

Albert shrugged. "Not particularly."

At this point, I didn't really suspect Albert of anything. All signs were pointing toward Vernon wandering off in the night.

"Maybe he got abducted by aliens," Albert said. "With any luck, that son-of-a-bitch is getting probed right now." He laughed at the thought.

I dug into my pocket and gave him a card. "If you hear from Vernon or see him around, give me a call."

Albert took the card with a twisted face, examined it for a moment, and set it on the end table next to the chair.

We left Albert's room and strolled through the maze of passageways to find Phyllis. If anybody might have some real intel, I figured it would be her.

8

"He didn't say anything to me," Phyllis said with a concerned look on her face.

She was in her mid-70s with elegant features. Her once full lips were now thin, and her face was crinkled and lined, but she still held the remnants of her former beauty. The sparkle in her blue eyes was still there. She had short silver hair and a stylish cut. She looked fit and trim and could grace the cover of a seniors' magazine.

"He's not at any of the usual locales," I said. "Can you think of anywhere else he might be?"

Her face tensed as she thought about it. "What about local restaurants? The Lobster Lounge. He likes that place. They have a seniors' buffet at 4:00 PM."

"I don't think Vernon would leave in the middle of the night for the buffet at the Lobster Lounge, but we'll look."

She frowned in agreement. "Well, he's not always in his right mind."

"So I've heard. When was the last time you saw Vernon?"

"Last night after dinner. I stopped by his room for a little company."

"How long were you there?"

She shrugged innocently. "Maybe an hour."

"What did you do?"

She smirked. "I don't see how that's any of your business."

I chuckled.

"Hey, the old guy's still got it. He may not remember who I am, but he remembers what to do with it." She lifted a sassy eyebrow.

JD and I were both amused. Phyllis was definitely the prize of Sunset Palms. It seemed like Vernon was getting more action than anybody else in here.

"Did he ever mention anything to you about trying to escape?"

"This isn't Alcatraz."

"You know what I mean," I said.

"Vernon has an adventurous spirit. I think he's still a kid at heart. Aren't we all? If there was anywhere he needed to escape from, it was his own mind. I feel like he's a prisoner inside there. Vernon is in there. He comes out sometimes. I tried walking him down memory lane, looking at old photographs, listening to old music. That seems to bring him around sometimes. But other times, he doesn't recognize me," she said with a disappointed head shake. She slumped, and sadness filled her eyes.

"Sounds like you two like each other."

She forced a somber smile, and her eyes misted. "We've had some good times. He's a kind, sensitive, caring man."

"What about Albert?"

"I like Albert, too, but in a different way. I wish those two would grow up and not be so contentious. Aren't we past that point? I mean, what does it really matter? I want to live for the moment. Go with the flow. Follow my heart wherever that may lead. It's not like any of us are at the beginning. It's a tough pill to swallow when you get to the point in your life where most of it is behind you. But at the same time, it's liberating in a way. You gotta make every second count. I, for one, am going to do whatever feels good. I've lived my life for too long, trying to please other people. It's time I please myself," she said, lifting her nose in the air with a hint of a smile and an optimistic gaze.

I gave her a card. "If you hear from Vernon or think of somewhere he might be, give me a call."

"I will, Deputy," she said with a flirty gaze, fluttering her eyelashes. "I'm sure he'll turn up somewhere. Have you checked the strip clubs?"

9

We left the Sunset Palms and drove around the neighborhood. We hit the Lobster Lounge, the Reef Shack, the Conch Brewery, and anything else that looked interesting.

There was no trace of Vernon.

"Maybe we should hit the strip club," JD said. "Strictly for investigative purposes."

I doubted that Vernon had made it all the way to Oyster Avenue and was hanging out in Forbidden Fruit. But there were worse places to look.

I called Paris Delaney, sent her Vernon's picture, and asked her to get the word out.

"No problem," she said. "I hope you find him." She paused for a moment before asking a favor of her own. "What can you tell me about the explosion at the warehouse yesterday?"

"It's a federal case. That's all I can really say."

"Are you investigating it?"

"We're doing our due diligence."

"Okay, now for the real story. Tell me more about JD running for mayor?"

I laughed. "I think he's really going to give it a go."

"So, he's serious?"

"Yes."

"As odd as this may sound, he's got my full support. We both know our current mayor is a crook. And to tell you the truth, Jim Brooks isn't much better."

"Do you still have that footage?" I asked.

She knew exactly what I was referring to. "You know I do. I have an archive of goodies that you would not believe. People would kill to get their hands on this."

"You should watch your back."

"Believe me, I keep my wits about me at all times. But if you want to watch my back, I wouldn't mind," she said in a naughty voice.

"What are your plans for the footage?"

"Are you asking me to release the footage just before the election in order to tip the scales in favor of your candidate?" she asked with mischief in her voice.

"I'm not asking you to do anything." I had a suspicion she planned on doing that all on her own.

"Of course, I will want exclusive and unprecedented access to the campaign. And during his tenure as mayor, I would expect the same access. Of course, all breaking news would flow through me first."

"Is that what you would expect?" I said with more than a trace of sarcasm.

"You scratch my back, I'll scratch yours."

"Did I tell you how much I hate politics?"

"Oh please, you're as good at the game as anybody else. Life is politics. Life is a negotiation. It's all a give-and-take. In some areas, it's just more overt than others."

She wasn't lying.

I asked Jack if he was willing to give Paris an interview.

"All day and twice on Sunday."

I relayed the message to Paris. "I'll let you two work out the details."

The grin on her face came through in her voice. "I'll be in touch."

She ended the call, and we drove across the island to find Monica. She lived in a little yellow bungalow on Tropic Palm Terrace. It was *way* out of the price range of a CNA's salary, but maybe she had inherited the home.

JD parked at the curb and we strolled the red brick walkway, through the picket fence, to the front porch. A few tall palms swayed overhead. The flowerbeds were vibrant with color.

I rang the video doorbell, and a voice crackled through the speaker a moment later. "Can I help you?"

I flashed my badge to the lens and made introductions.

"We just need a brief word with you."

"What's this about?"

"Vernon has gone missing."

"Oh, my goodness. I'll be right there."

The line disconnected.

JD and I waited on the porch for a few minutes until Monica pulled open the door. She was a pear-shaped woman in her mid-30s with straight brownish-blonde hair with streaks of frosting that hung to her shoulders. She wore jeans and a T-shirt. Concern filled her eyes. "What happened? Did he just walk out of the facility?"

"We believe so," I said.

"What time?"

"I'm not really sure. Sometime in the night. When was the last time you saw him?"

She thought about it for a moment. "At bed check. That was around 9:00 PM. You can check the logs."

"We did."

"Did you see him after that?"

She shook her head.

"What time did you get off shift?"

"3:00 AM."

"Is that typical for you?"

She nodded. "Right now, I'm on nights. But we rotate."

"Was Vernon prone to getting up in the middle of the night and wandering around?"

"Occasionally, I'd catch him wandering the halls. He'd get disoriented at times. Sometimes he'd think it was breakfast at 3:00 AM. He suffers from cognitive issues."

"We know."

"You know that this isn't the first time he's disappeared," she said.

I nodded, and she proceeded to tell me what we already learned.

"The entrances and exits are all access controlled. The front desk will get an alert if a door is opened to the facility. But sometimes that can go unnoticed. Especially in the wee hours of the morning." Then she shrugged innocently. "I'm not saying anyone regularly falls asleep on the job." But that's exactly what she was saying. Her face tensed with worry. "I do hope he's okay."

"I'm sure he'll turn up," I said. "We've got everyone looking for him."

"Please keep me posted if he turns up."

"I will." I gave her a card. "Get in touch if you see or hear from him."

She nodded, took the card, and slid back inside.

JD and I walked back to the Porsche and climbed in.

"Are you hungry?" JD asked.

"I could eat."

We cruised up to Oyster Avenue, found a place to park, then strolled the sidewalk until we found a place to suit our fancy. We grabbed a bite to eat at the Driftwood Diner. I went with the Driftwood Bacon Cheeseburger, and Jack had the tangy shrimp tacos.

The place had a colorful, beachy vibe, with paintings of seascapes and sailboats. The tables and booths were fashioned to look like they were made of driftwood. We'd hardly taken a few bites when the sheriff called.

I answered with a mouthful. "Did you find Vernon?"

"No. We've got another situation."

"Can this wait? We just sat down to lunch."

"Oh, I'm sorry. I didn't mean to interrupt," he snarked. Then he barked, "Get your asses down here!"

10

An ambulance pulled away from the scene as we arrived, lights flashing. The siren spun up.

A crowd of curious onlookers had gathered. Now that the excitement was over, they began to disperse.

Lights flashed and flickered atop patrol cars.

Blood stained the sidewalk.

Dietrich snapped photos, and forensic investigators scoured the area.

JD pulled to the curb behind the sheriff's patrol car. We hopped out and joined him on the bloodstained sidewalk.

"What happened?" I asked, having a pretty good idea already.

"Drive-by shooting," Daniels said. "Kid was still breathing, but barely."

"Got an ID on the victim?"

"Lamonte Kent."

"Any witnesses?"

"Nobody's talking. They never do around here."

This wasn't the greatest part of town. The corner of Dowling and Jefferson was well known for its chaos. This was the place you could find just about anything you wanted and some things you didn't. Drugs, prostitutes... Dowling Street had it all.

I glanced around, looking for any surveillance cameras, but didn't see any. Cameras didn't last long in this part of town. Somebody would take a baseball bat to them or spray-paint the lenses. This wasn't the kind of place where you wanted a video record of your activities.

"Drug-related?" I asked.

"Or gang related. Take your pick. Kid had a pocket full of dope on him. Heroin, cocaine, crack. He had a lot of cash, including several crisp hundred-dollar bills. You tell me what he was doing on the street corner," the sheriff said with a hint of sarcasm.

A few stray bullets had missed their target and chipped the concrete of the red brick building on the corner. Dietrich snapped photos of a bullet embedded in the mortar, then forensic investigators went about recovering the slug.

It was about noon. This had happened within the last hour or so.

When the traffic cleared, I hustled across the street to a convenience store. JD followed along. The bell chimed as we stepped inside. I flashed my badge as I approached the counter.

The clerk was an older gentleman with dark hair, narrow brown eyes, and a weathered face. He was probably late 50s, early 60s. The bulletproof glass insulated him from the chaos somewhat. From the register, he would have had a clear view across the street.

"You happen to see anything?"

He shook his head.

"Come on. A kid gets gunned down right across the street from you, and you don't see or hear anything?"

"Not my problem. Besides, it's one less criminal to deal with. Let them kill each other."

"Innocent people could get killed in the crossfire."

He frowned at me. "I got robbed five times in the last two months." He tapped on the glass. "You know how much this cost to install? If you guys would do a better job, maybe there wouldn't be somebody selling dope on every corner around here. They sell that shit to little kids, you know?"

"I'm aware."

"I guarantee you, in a half-hour, somebody else will be there to take his place," the clerk said.

"So the kid was selling dope?"

The clerk nodded.

"He's a regular on this corner?"

He nodded again.

"What's your name?"

"David Chen."

I didn't see any shell casings at the scene. The spent cartridges were probably still within the shooter's vehicle. "What type of car was the shooter driving?"

David hesitated a moment. "A silver four-door sedan."

"Did you get a license plate?"

He shook his head.

"Did you see the driver?"

"No."

"How long have you been working here?"

"I own the store. I've owned it for 20 years. I've watched this place go from a decent neighborhood to an absolute shit hole. I shouldn't have to spend all day behind glass. I shouldn't have to watch people die in the streets. My family shouldn't be in danger."

I looked around the store.

There was a surveillance camera aimed at the front door. I thought maybe there was a chance it had captured the chaos across the street.

The store had a typical layout with rows and rows of snacks, candy, bags of chips, doughnuts, and toiletries. In the back freezer there was beer, soda, milk, and bottled water. A warmer against the far wall offered pizza by the slice.

"You mind if we take a look at the security footage?"

He hesitated for a moment. David really didn't want to get involved. I didn't blame him. He'd risk retaliation. He lived in this neighborhood. He wasn't a tourist like the rest of us. We were just here for the carnage.

"Help us find the shooter, and that will be one less dangerous person on the streets," I said.

11

David locked the doors, then showed us to the back office and pulled up the footage from the camera. It was positioned in the ceiling and had a clear view of the register and the door but didn't catch the opposite side of the street.

There was nothing to see.

I thanked him for his cooperation, gave him a card, then we hustled back across the street to join the sheriff. By that time, the crowd had moved on to other things.

Paris Delaney had arrived, but there wasn't much happening. The cameraman filmed the bloodstained sidewalk, along with the chips in the brick from the bullets. Paris interviewed a few people who remained on the scene, but they didn't have much to add.

Her cameraman closed in on us as we returned.

"Deputy Wild, what can you tell us about this incident?"

I didn't know any more than she did and made my usual plea for any witnesses to come forward.

After I stepped off-camera, Daniels said, "Get to the hospital and talk to the kid, if he makes it."

"We're on it," I said.

We hopped into the Porsche and hustled back across the island to Coconut General. The waiting room was full of the walking dead. I talked to the receptionist and told her to have Dr. Parker talk to me at his earliest convenience. We took a seat and caught a replay of Paris's on-scene report.

It wasn't long before a distraught woman burst into the ER with frantic eyes. She hurried to the receptionist with her 14-year-old son trailing behind her. She asked about Lamonte.

I sprang from my seat and made my way toward her, flashing my badge. "I'm Deputy Wild with Coconut County."

Her eyes filled, and her face contorted with sorrow. "Is he going to be okay?"

"That's a question for the doctors. I'm sure they're doing everything they can. He's in good hands here."

Her son clutched her hand as she did everything she could not to lose it.

"I know this is a difficult time. I need to ask you a few questions."

She sniffled, grabbed a tissue from her purse, and blotted her eyes.

"Drugs and a substantial amount of cash were found on him," I said. "How long had he been dealing?"

She hesitated, and her face tightened. "I don't know anything about that."

Something told me she knew *all* about that.

"I need you to be honest with me. It's the only way we can find out who attempted to kill your son."

A grim frown tightened her face.

"We think this could have been a rival gang, another drug dealer, or perhaps an angry customer. Did Lamonte have a beef with anyone?"

Ms. Kent frowned. "I don't know. I can tell you he ran with the wrong crowd. I've already lost two children to the streets. I'm not going to lose a third." She looked at her son. "Don't you dare get involved in this shit, you hear me?"

He nodded with the fear of God in his eyes.

"You said he ran with the wrong crowd. Is he in a gang?"

"I don't know. He doesn't tell me anything."

"Who does he hang out with?"

"Jaxon is his best friend."

"Does he have a girlfriend?"

"They just broke up, I think. I can't keep up. Her name is April."

"I'll need contact info for her and Jaxon."

She nodded, sniffled, and blotted her eyes again.

I addressed her young son. "And what's your name?"

He exchanged a wary glance with his mother before answering.

"It's okay. Answer the man."

"Will," he said.

It was easy to see he had an inherent distrust of cops.

"Was Lamonte worried about anyone coming after him?"

Will shrugged.

"How long had he been dealing?"

"Since he was my age, at least. Mom couldn't pay the rent until Lamonte started helping out."

"William!"

The kid shrugged. "What? It's true."

She dismissed him. "It is not." She looked at me with guilty eyes. "I didn't need anything from anyone. And I most certainly wouldn't put one of my children on the streets, dealing drugs."

She may not have put Lamonte on the street corner, but she knew damn good and well where the money came from.

I asked Will, "What gang is he affiliated with?"

The boy hesitated a moment. "The Ruthless Killers." Then he added, "But you didn't hear that shit from me."

"William!" his mother scolded.

He looked at her like she was crazy. He wasn't used to getting chastised for his language.

"I didn't raise my boys to be hoodlums," she assured.

"You know where I can find these Ruthless Killers?"

William shrugged.

I gave them both a card. "Please get in contact if you need anything or if any details come to light."

She gave me the numbers for Lamonte's ex-girlfriend, April, and Jaxon. Then JD and I returned to our seats.

Lamonte was in surgery for hours. The receptionist finally called Ms. Kent to the desk.

Dr. Parker emerged from the double doors a few moments later and joined her. JD and I hustled across the waiting room.

"He is in stable condition," Parker said.

Ms. Kent breathed a sigh of relief. "Oh, thank God!"

"He'll be in a critical care unit for several days. He got lucky."

"Can I see him?"

"He's pretty groggy right now, but you can poke your head in for a minute." Parker glanced at us. "No questions today. He wouldn't be able to answer them, anyway. He's pretty medicated. Come back tomorrow."

I thanked him for the info. We said our goodbyes to Ms. Kent, then left the ER and walked across the parking lot to the Porsche.

Lamonte would have a long road ahead of him, but at least he was alive.

We set out to find Jaxon, but that would be no easy task.

12

———

According to the DMV records, Jaxon lived with his mother in an apartment in Jamaica Village. It was a dreary part of town. The kind of place where hopes and dreams were crushed. The kind of place you struggled to get out of, and if you ever did, you never came back.

We parked at the curb on Colton Street, climbed out, and strode the walkway to unit #3B. I put a heavy fist against the door.

Commotion inside filtered down the foyer.

The Excalibur wasn't much to speak of. It was a dumpy little strip of units in the shadows of towering power lines. The Tudor-style building with brown trim stood out like a sore thumb among the tropical motifs on the island.

"Who is it?" a woman shouted from within.

"Coconut County," I said. "We need to speak with Jaxon."

"What's this about?"

I told her.

"Lamonte was shot?"

"Yes, ma'am."

She paused for a long moment. "Jaxon's not here right now."

She knew not to open the door for cops. I suspected this wasn't the first time deputies had knocked on her door.

"Do you know where he is?" I asked.

"He's not in any trouble, is he?"

"No, ma'am. We're just hoping he may have information about Lamonte's shooters."

"Is Lamonte okay?"

"He's been better. But the outlook is promising."

"I don't know where Jaxon is," she said. "I can never keep up with him."

"Where does he usually hang out?"

"Like I said, I really don't know. And he doesn't tell me."

I doubted she was telling the truth. I didn't think she knew *everything* Jaxon was into, but she wasn't offering anything useful.

"I'm going to leave my card outside the door. When Jaxon returns, would you have him get in touch with me?"

"I'll let him know you stopped by."

That was about the best I could hope for.

We thanked her for her time, then made our way back to the Porsche.

We drove to April's apartment a few blocks over, but she wasn't there either. Her mother told us we could find her at work. JD drove to the Coconut Key Pharmacy and caught up with her at the makeup counter. Fear drenched her face when I flashed my badge. "I did not hit that woman's car. I don't care what she says."

JD and I exchanged a curious glance.

"We're not here about a hit-and-run," I said.

Her face wrinkled with confusion. "Then why are you here?"

I told her that Lamonte had been shot.

Her jaw dropped, then she gave a nonchalant shrug. "I warned him."

"What did you warn him about?"

"That boy was playing with fire," she said.

"Care to elaborate?"

"He messed with the wrong girl."

"Is that why you two broke up?"

"Hell, yes," she said. "I ain't got time for that."

"Whose girl did he mess with?"

"Mario's girl, Esmerelda."

"Who's Mario?"

"He's the leader of the Blood Demons. I told Lamonte, you're gonna get shot doing stuff like that." She gave another nonchalant shrug. "I guess I was right."

"You don't seem upset about it at all," I said.

"Why should I care about someone who clearly didn't care about me?"

"Do you know where we can find Esmeralda?"

She gave us a look. One that told me she didn't think too highly of Esmeralda or her chosen profession. "She works at the Pussycat Palace."

It was a totally nude strip club on the outskirts of town.

"Mario must not be a jealous man if he lets his girlfriend work in a place like that," I said.

"There's a difference between men paying to see your woman naked and sticking your hotdog where it don't belong."

She had a point.

"You know where we can find Mario?"

She shrugged again.

"Was there anyone else who had a beef with Lamonte?"

"I don't know. I'm sure he pissed off a lot of people."

"Why do you say that?"

"He wasn't loyal to me. Maybe he wasn't loyal to anybody else, either. Once a cheater, always a cheater."

"I'm guessing you were pretty mad at Lamonte."

"Oh, no. I was thrilled," she said, thick with sarcasm. "I just love it when my man goes out and sleeps with some skanky ho. No telling what he picked up."

"Maybe you wanted a little payback."

She lifted a sassy eyebrow. "You think I shot Lamonte?"

I shrugged.

"How long have you been on shift today?"

"I came in at 10:00 AM." She paused. "Let me tell you something. If I wanted payback, I'd have shot him in the balls. Was he shot in the balls?"

"I don't know the exact location of his injuries."

"If there's any karma, he'd have been shot in the balls." She paused, then softened. "Is he gonna make it?"

"He's in stable condition," I said. "You know where we can find Jaxon?"

"If he's not on the street corner, slanging rock, then you might be able to find him at Sharkfin or Anton's place."

"Who's Anton?"

"He runs the Ruthless Killers." April rolled her eyes. "They like to think of themselves as this big, badass gang. But there are only six of them." She laughed.

"What about the Blood Demons? How big of an organization are they?"

"There are at least 20 of them." April shook her head. "I told him that's like stirring up a hornets' nest."

"Do you think Anton and his crew might retaliate?"

13

———

"They have to," April said. "They'll look weak if they don't. The whole thing is stupid, if you ask me. I don't see why they can't just agree to divvy up the territory. They're all nickel-and-diming, anyway."

"So there was tension before Lamonte hooked up with Esmeralda?"

"There's always tension. I don't need to tell you how it is on the streets."

"You seem like you've got a good head on your shoulders," I said. "How did you get hooked up with Lamonte in the first place?"

She softened for a moment as she thought about it. "I don't know. I guess I was young and stupid. He was cute and charming. Or so I thought."

She was still young.

"When did you first start dating?"

"Last year. And I've learned a lot in that timeframe."

I gave her my card and thanked her for the info, then I talked to her manager and confirmed that she had punched in on time.

We left the pharmacy and headed back to Dowling Street to look for Jaxon. We cruised the infamous boulevard and found him on the exact corner where Lamonte had been doing business. Jack pulled to the curb, and Jaxon approached. He was a big guy with a barrel chest. He stood about 6'2" with a curly beard.

I figured he was proving a point. He wouldn't be scared off his turf.

"What do you need?" he asked as he stepped to the window.

There were only a few things guys in a Porsche needed in this part of town. Information wasn't usually one of them.

"Need to talk to you about Lamonte," I said.

"You 5-O?"

I flashed the badge.

Without hesitation, he bolted. His feet sprouted wings, and he was gone. Jaxon rounded the corner and didn't look back.

Jack launched the Porsche after him, banking a hard right. He pulled alongside Jaxon, pacing him.

"I just need to talk," I shouted.

Jaxon wasn't having any of it.

He veered up a driveway, pushed through a back gate, and disappeared.

"Go get him," Jack shouted.

"You go get him."

He frowned at me, stomped the gas, and blazed down the street to the next intersection. He took a right at the stop sign, then another right, hoping to bump into Jaxon on the next street over.

We rounded the corner just in time to see the big guy dart across the street. He saw us and sprinted up another driveway.

Jack barreled down the street just as Jaxon disappeared into another backyard.

I hopped out and gave chase. By the time I ran up the driveway and into the backyard, Jaxon was over the fence. He was pretty quick for a big guy.

Dogs barked as he tore across the yard and burst through the gate, the dogs nipping at his heels.

As I pulled myself up, the Dobermans turned their attention to me. They raced across the backyard and leaped onto the fence, snapping and snarling. I got a face full of glistening fangs and bad doggie breath.

I wanted to talk to Jaxon, but not that bad. I figured we'd catch up with him later.

"What the hell are you doing on my property?" a man behind me yelled.

The question was followed by the unmistakable clack of a pump-action shotgun.

I lowered myself down, put my hands in the air, and turned around with caution. "I'm a Deputy with Coconut County."

"Let's see your badge!"

He was a fit guy in his mid-60s with white hair and a trimmed beard. Living around here, he was no stranger to shenanigans. I figured this wasn't the first time he'd pulled a shotgun on an intruder.

"It's in my pocket," I said, slowly reaching.

"Don't try anything funny."

I chuckled and carefully slid my credentials from my pocket.

He squinted as the gold badge gleamed in the Florida sunshine. Satisfied, he lowered the weapon. "What the hell are you doing?"

"Chasing a suspect."

"What'd he do?"

"I just need to talk to him."

"This place is going to hell in a handbasket. Why don't you do something?"

"We're trying," I assured.

"Try harder."

With that, we said our goodbyes, and I hustled back to the street.

JD was gone. I figured he'd spun around the block, looking for Jaxon.

The roar of the flat-six echoed from the next block over. It wasn't long before he rounded the corner and pulled alongside me. I hopped in, and he gave me grief. "What happened?"

"He got away."

Jack frowned. "You're losing it."

I rolled my eyes.

"Well, I guess that leaves us no choice but to go to the Pussycat Palace and find Esmeralda."

14

I didn't even know if she was working, but we were about to find out. We stepped into the dim club as sultry music pumped through the speakers. A flash of the badge got us past the bouncer and the cashier.

If Forbidden Fruit was a nice French Grand Cru, the Pussycat Palace was box wine. It got the job done, but there was nothing fancy about it.

Bart ran the place, and we found him at the bar. He was in his 70s with a Mohawk that was dyed green. He wore a T-shirt with the sleeves cut out and cargo shorts. He had a swarthy tan, and his biceps bulged. He was fit and trim and could probably whoop the snot out of the mouthy 20-year-olds that frequented the joint. He spent a lot of time out on the water, and it showed on his skin.

I flashed my badge as we approached. We'd been in a few times before, but I figured I'd jog his memory. "Looking for Esmeralda. I don't know her stage name."

"Destiny. At least that's what I think she's going by lately." He squinted and surveyed the club. He pointed to a gorgeous brunette across the club, tantalizing a young man with her endowments. "She in some kind of trouble?"

"No trouble at all. We just need to ask her a few questions."

"Don't interrupt her while she's doing business."

"Fair enough. Have the waitress send her over when she's finished. We'll find ourselves a seat."

Bart didn't extend quite the same hospitality to us as Jacko did at Forbidden Fruit, but at least he was cooperative.

JD and I took a seat at a table not far from the main stage.

The DJ's voice boomed through the speakers. "Please welcome to the stage, Charity."

The delightful blonde pranced down the stage, wearing frilly black lingerie complete with thigh-high stockings and a garter belt. Seductive music pumped through speakers, and she slinked around a chrome pole, teasing the audience with her supple curves. It wasn't long before she started dismantling her outfit in the most alluring of ways. She unclasped her bra, let the straps dangle from her shoulders, then she shimmied out of the garment and bounced free.

There was much rejoicing.

Then she worked on the garter belt.

Then, the stockings, one by one, making it look effortless.

It wasn't long after before she slithered those lacy panties down her smooth thighs.

Men threw dollar bills on stage and soaked up the perfection of her form.

Charity delighted the audience for a few minutes, then the song ended. She gathered her garments and slinked off the stage to get dressed again. From there, she would work the floor, looking for more lucrative encounters.

JD and I were forced to sit through performances from Crystal, Danica, Star, and Chardonnay. It was brutal. Hard work. But we were brave.

Esmeralda finally made her way over to our table. She plopped down in an empty chair and surveyed us with cautious eyes. "Bart says you want to talk to me. What's this about?"

"It's about Lamonte," I said.

"What about him?"

"He's in the hospital right now with a few holes in him."

Her eyes filled with surprise. "What does that have to do with me?"

"You two were close, weren't you?"

"No," she said with a wrinkled face.

"No? That's not what I hear."

"Well, you heard wrong, Mister."

I gave her a flat look. "You two didn't have a casual hookup?"

"No." There was that wrinkled face again.

15

I just stared at her.

"What does it matter, anyway?"

"I get it. You don't want your boyfriend to find out."

A guilty frown tugged Esmeralda's face. "Where did you hear this from?"

"I've got my sources."

She glanced around, leaned in, and spoke in a hushed tone. "Mario would kill me if he found out."

"We're just talking here. It's just between us." I paused. "Have you considered the fact that Mario already knows? I mean, maybe he's the one who shot Lamonte?"

Fear filled her eyes. "He'd beat me senseless."

"Sounds like a real nice guy. What are you doing with him?"

She shrugged.

"Surely a woman like you could do better," I said.

"I could do a lot better," she replied with a sassy voice.

"Why don't you leave?"

"Because Mario would track me down and kill me. That's why."

"He sounds just like the type of guy who would gun down a man who messed with his woman."

Esmeralda nodded.

"Do you know where Mario was this morning?"

"I came into work about 10:00 AM. The buffet can get pretty busy. Sometimes, I can make more money during the day than I can at night."

"Was Mario with you until you came in?"

She nodded.

That certainly didn't rule him out.

I dug into my pocket, pulled out a card, and placed it on the table. "Call me if you hear anything."

"I ain't no snitch."

"Sounds to me like you might be in danger. If Mario killed Lamonte, you might be next."

She didn't like the sound of that, but she knew it was true.

"Any idea where we can find him?"

Esmeralda hesitated for a moment. She looked around the club, then said, "He's at his shop. Eastside Island Customs." Then she added, "He loves cars more than he loves me."

74TRIPP ELLIS

"You know where Mario was between 10:00 AM and noon today?"

She shook her head.

I thanked her for her time. JD and I stood up.

Esmeralda had a nervous look on her face. "What are you going to do?"

"We're going to have a little talk with Mario."

"You can't tell him anything about me and Lamonte!" Panic filled her eyes.

"I won't bring it up," I said. "But if he talks about it, it's fair game."

She hesitated a moment. "If he already knows, will you call me and tell me?"

I said I would.

"I'm going to give you my number, okay?" She grabbed my card from the table, sent me a text, and my phone buzzed a moment later.

I pulled it from my pocket and saved her in my contact list.

We said our goodbyes, then talked to Bart on the way out. He confirmed that Esmeralda had been at the club since 10:00 AM.

We left the strip club and stepped into the bright Florida sunshine that squinted our eyes. JD and I strolled across the lot, hopped into the Porsche, and cruised across the island with the top down. It was a beautiful day, and the wind swirled. '80s rock blasted through the speakers.

It only took a few minutes to reach our destination. Jack pulled into the lot of Eastside Island Customs. The grounds were surrounded by a chain-link fence topped by concertina wire.

If you were into hot rods, this was the place to be.

There were custom-modded cars with flame paint jobs, sparkling metallic flake, hood scoops, and chrome exhausts. Inside one of the bay doors, a shower of golden sparks flew as one of the technicians used a disk sander on a piece of metal. The sound buzzed the air, and the smell of hot metal swirled.

JD's Ruby Star 911 looked out of place here, but the bold color still stood out among the hot rods.

We hopped out and walked toward one of the open bays. There were a couple cars on lifts inside. This was the perfect place to launder money for a small, would-be gang.

A guy with a shaved head, brown eyes, and a mustache and goatee approached. He wore a white ribbed tank top and khaki shorts, all of which were covered in grease. Monochrome tattoos sleeved his arms with several gang-related designs.

By the car we were driving, we certainly weren't one of the usual customers. His suspicious eyes surveyed us. "What do you want?"

Not the ideal way to greet a customer.

"You Mario?" I asked.

"Who's asking?"

I flashed my badge, and his face tensed.

"Just wondering if you heard the news," I said.

"What news?"

"Lamonte Kent has been shot."

He shrugged. "So?"

"Just thought you might have an opinion on that."

"Why would I?"

I shrugged.

"He's associated with the Ruthless Killers."

"What does that have to do with me?"

I gave him a flat look.

"I'm a legitimate businessman. As you can see, I run a clean shop. The best custom work on the island."

"Really nice work," JD said.

Mario wasn't exactly sure how to respond to the compliment. JD's praise was sincere.

Mario paused for a moment, sizing Jack up. "We can turn your car into something special."

Jack chuckled. "I think it's pretty special already."

"Nice, but kinda plain. We could add a little spice to it. You seem like a guy that likes a little spice."

Jack was no stranger to the outrageous. "What would you do to it?"

Mario surveyed the car for a moment. "Needs to be lowered. I like the paint, but it needs a custom touch. We could flare the fenders. It definitely needs a wing on the back. More aggressive aero on the front."

"I think I'll keep it stock for now," Jack said.

"Don't be boring. Live a little. Be unique. Stand out from the crowd."

Jack chuckled. "I'll consider it."

"You're pretty dialed into the street," I said. "Have you heard anything about Lamonte?" I studied his face, looking for a reaction.

"Why do you think I'm dialed into the street?"

I shrugged.

"Like I said, I'm a legitimate businessman."

I nodded, going along with it. "Right. Of course."

We stood there for a moment, staring at each other. I found if you let the silence go on long enough, it would get so uncomfortable that people would usually start talking. Even when they didn't want to. Something to fill the void. Anything but silence.

"If that's all, I'm really busy," Mario said. "I need to get back to work."

"Have you been here all day?"

"Since 9 o'clock this morning."

"Can anybody else verify that?"

His eyes narrowed at me. "Why are you so curious, man?"

"Just trying to rule you out as a suspect."

His face wrinkled. "Why would I be a suspect? I hardly know the guy."

"So, you do know him?"

"Yeah, I know who he is. I know everybody."

"See. Dialed into the street."

He frowned, then yelled back into the garage. "Hey, Pablo. Have I been here all day?"

"Yeah," Pablo said.

"See," he said in triumph. "I didn't shoot nobody."

I stared him down again for another long moment.

"It ain't me you're looking for," Mario said. "I think Lamonte might have problems within his own crew."

"Why do you say that?"

16

Mario shrugged. "I hear Lamonte likes to talk."

"Talk trash?" I said.

His face wrinkled, and he looked at me like I was an idiot. "I hear he likes to talk to cops."

"An informant?"

"You say informant, I say snitch. And you know what happens to snitches."

"So, you think somebody in the Ruthless Killers took him out?"

"I don't know nothing. But if I was a cop, that's where I'd look."

My eyes narrowed with suspicion. I figured Mario would say just about anything to get us off his back. But he hadn't shown any signs of anger toward Lamonte.

I got the impression Mario was a guy who wore his emotions on his sleeve. I don't think he'd have been able to hide his disdain if he knew Lamonte had been diddling his girlfriend.

I gave him a card and told him to get in touch if he heard anything else that might be of interest.

"Think about it," Mario said to Jack as we walked back to the Porsche.

I called Denise.

The delightful redhead answered after a few rings, and her silky voice filtered through the line. "Hey, I was just about to call you."

"Always on your mind."

"Dream on."

"What's up?" I asked.

"You first."

"Can you tell me if Lamonte Kent is listed as a confidential informant?"

Her fingers tapped the keys, and she replied a moment later. "He's not in the database."

"Interesting," I said.

She asked, and I gave her the scoop.

"I'll check with the other agencies," she said. "Maybe he's working with the DEA."

After our last investigation, we weren't on the best of terms with the local DEA agents.

"You two need to get down here and take a look at this," she continued. "I'm about to call the treasury department."

"What's going on?"

"Some of the bills that Lamonte was in possession of are counterfeit."

I lifted a curious eyebrow. "How did you figure that out?"

"I think you'll be proud of me," she said with a smile in her voice. "I was logging in his property. Along with the cocaine, heroin, and methamphetamines that were found in his pockets, he had a substantial wad of cash. I was counting it out, and I noticed something really odd about the hundreds. The serial numbers didn't match the issuing Federal Reserve bank. Most people don't realize that each bank has its own designator. Whoever made these bills must have overlooked it. But I'll tell you, this is quality work. I'm no expert. But it's got the watermark, glow strip, and is printed on the right paper. You know how hard that paper is to come by?"

I was well aware.

It was a cotton and linen blend with embedded fibers. If you asked a paper company to make something like that, they knew exactly what you were trying to do.

"We're on our way," I said.

JD spun the car around, and we hustled to the station. We met up with Denise in the property department, and she showed us the bills.

I was no expert, but these bills were almost indistinguishable from real currency. I held it up to the light and looked for the watermark. Then I examined it with an ultraviolet flashlight.

It passed all the tests.

The only way to determine these were fake was due to the incorrect serial numbers. Even then, the average person wouldn't pick up on it.

"Where the hell do you think Lamonte got these?" JD asked.

I shrugged. "Maybe he got them from a customer?"

"I think we need to have a little talk with him."

"I'll call the hospital and see if he's up to taking visitors," Denise said.

It wasn't long before Agent Foster showed up. Denise had contacted her. Foster looked quite a bit different from the last time I had seen her. She covered the scuffs and scrapes on her face with makeup for the most part, and she looked pretty well put together in that navy pantsuit of hers.

"I'm surprised to see you back on duty so soon," I said.

"What was I going to do? Sit around and let Viktor Nevsky carry on, business as usual?"

"I like your spirit."

She gave me a flat look, not impressed by my attempt at flattery. "It has nothing to do with spirit. My partner is dead, and I want blood."

"Like I said, I like your spirit."

"Let's see what you've got," she said.

I showed her the counterfeit bills, and she examined them carefully. Foster seemed impressed. "This is good. Real good. Tell me how you came across these again."

I gave her the scoop.

"And the kid in possession of these is sitting in the hospital right now?"

I nodded.

"I want to talk with him ASAP."

Denise rejoined us. "Just got off the phone with the hospital. Lamonte is still in critical care. No visitors."

"Is he going to make it?" Olivia asked.

Denise shrugged.

"He could be our only link to the counterfeiter. I guarantee this is why Viktor is in town."

"Counterfeiting doesn't seem to be in his wheelhouse," I said. I told her my theory about Lamonte possibly taking money from a client.

Confusion tensed Foster's face. "Doesn't make a lot of sense. Why pass counterfeit bills around town? That's not something I would do, especially if I had a buyer like Nevsky on the line. I wouldn't circulate the bills at all. I wouldn't want to raise any flags. I'd move all the money at once and let him take them overseas and resell them. Hundred-dollar bills are more scrutinized than other denominations of currency. It's easier to pass 20s."

"Maybe our counterfeiter wanted to test the waters," JD said.

"We don't know how many people those bills passed through before they got to Lamonte."

Special Agent Foster considered it.

Jack looked at his watch. With an optimistic grin, he said, "It's almost happy hour. Maybe we should discuss this further over drinks?"

Agent Foster was not enthused about the idea. "I'm sorry, but I have work to do. Thanks for the heads up. If you come across any more of these bills, please get in touch with me." She logged out the evidence and left the station.

"She's not very friendly," JD muttered.

"She just hasn't warmed up to us yet."

Denise rolled her eyes. "I don't think she's going to warm up to either of you."

I laughed. "Do I detect a note of jealousy?"

"In your dreams," she said as she moseyed away.

JD and I watched her saunter down the hallway. She certainly had a nice saunter.

"I was thinking we could grab a few drinks and a bite to eat at Wetsuit, then we could hit that gallery show. Free drinks, hors d'oeuvres... How can we go wrong? Plus, Shawna wasn't bad to look at."

"Sasha," I clarified.

"Whatever. Close enough."

I chuckled.

We left the station and headed up to Oyster Avenue. We indulged in a few culinary delights at Wetsuit, had a few drinks, and took in the sumptuous scenery of scantily clad waitresses in tight neoprene jackets and skimpy bikini bottoms. We kicked around theories about the cases.

After we filled our bellies, we left and headed over to the gallery.

But we were a little too late.

Just as we arrived, two masked thugs darted out of the gallery with what looked like bags full of loot. They wore hats and sunglasses. Bandanas covered their faces. They hopped into a black sedan and screeched out of the parking lot.

JD stomped the gas and gave chase.

17

J D mashed the pedal to the floor, and the engine roared. The acceleration thrust me against the seat. I fumbled for my phone and dialed dispatch. I told them we were in pursuit, gave them a location, and asked them to send backup.

The black sedan pulled onto the main thoroughfare. We caught up to it in a heartbeat. The little four-cylinder was no match for the GTS.

They barreled down Sandy Shoal, which was a two-lane road with a double yellow line down the center. It had wide shoulders with parked cars.

We flew past storefronts, restaurants, and gift shops.

I'm sure it took the thugs a few moments to figure out why a Porsche was chasing them.

A slower car ahead of them impeded their progress. The black sedan veered across the double yellow line into the oncoming lane, passing the slower car. Horns honked, and oncoming lights flashed. The black sedan veered back into the lane just in time to miss the oncoming car. They came millimeters from clipping the front bumper of the slower car.

The slower car, now behind the sedan, jammed on their brakes. Red lights lit up, and JD stomped on the brakes to avoid collision.

The thugs banked a hard left at the next intersection, cutting off more traffic.

Tires squealed, and more horns honked.

JD followed when we reached the intersection.

The four-door sedan blasted down the street, then took a hard right at the stop sign. Tires squealed through the intersection.

JD stomped the pedal again, and it didn't take long for us to zip down the street. He turned at the stop sign just in time to see the thugs take a left at the next intersection.

As we rounded the next corner, a silver SUV backed out of a driveway, blocking the road. The driver didn't even bother to look.

JD slammed on the brakes and honked the horn.

The blonde woman behind the wheel flipped him off.

Jack kept on the horn, which did little to motivate the woman to move out of the way.

Finally, she put the SUV into gear and drove around the Porsche. She rolled the window down and told Jack off.

By this time, the black sedan was gone.

JD tore down the street and took a right at the next intersection, hoping we might get lucky.

We didn't see any trace of the thug's vehicle.

Jack spun the car around and headed back to the gallery. Patrol units were on the scene by the time we arrived. Red and blue lights flickered.

JD found a place to park. We hopped out and hustled into the gallery.

The patrons all looked frazzled.

Everyone was dressed to the nines. Elegant evening gowns and shimmering fabric. Hair in perfectly sculpted updos. Black tuxedos and bow ties.

But the sparkly accessories were conspicuously missing.

There was no glittering jewelry around smooth collarbones. No diamonds hanging from tender earlobes. No Rolexes on wrists.

JD and I were quite underdressed for the occasion.

Sasha talked to Mendoza and Robinson. Her eyes found me, and she rushed to greet us. "Oh, thank God you're here," she said, still trembling from the chaos.

"We tried to chase the assailants down, but they got away," I said.

She frowned. "It was terrible. They stormed in. One shot into the ceiling, then demanded everyone's jewelry. I mean, thank God no one was hurt, but the evening is ruined." A frown tensed her pretty lips.

"Can you give me a description of the assailants?"

"Well, you saw them, didn't you?"

"I'd like to get your version."

She described the perps and said that one was a little shorter than the other.

"Did you notice anything specific about them? Any identifiable features?"

Her face tightened as she thought about it for a moment. "One of them had a tribal tattoo on the back of his neck. It poked up above his collar, like wings spreading. I didn't really get a good look at it."

It was the same description of the goons that had robbed Diver Down not long ago. These guys had been knocking off restaurants around town, collecting wallets and jewelry from patrons. It seemed they had moved up to art galleries. Probably more lucrative. A higher-end clientele. Judging by the type of people here and the typical jewelry that was worn at swanky events like this, the robbers could have made off with millions.

A young man about Sasha's age hovered nearby. He had long, curly hair that hung into his face. He was slim, and the tuxedo he wore didn't appear to be the same cut or quality as most of the others in the room.

Sasha noticed my observation of him. "Deputy Wild, I'd like you to meet my friend, Nolan."

We shook hands and exchanged pleasantries.

"We've known each other since art school. Nolan is quite a talented artist. You really ought to see some of his work."

Nolan smiled. "She's just being kind. Sasha always was the gifted one."

"Well, I don't feel very gifted at the moment. Not a single piece of my artwork has sold this evening, and I don't expect it to. Not after this. Who's got money left?"

I couldn't tell if the two were an item, but I didn't get that vibe.

Mendoza and Robinson interviewed the guests and helped them walk through the process of filing a police report online. Through the portal, they could document their losses.

"I've already given a statement to the deputies," Nolan said. "If you don't mind, I'm going to sneak out. This whole thing has me kind of freaked out."

He gave Sasha a hug, then excused himself.

"Your boyfriend's gonna leave at a time like this?" JD said, fishing.

"He's not my boyfriend."

Jack gave me a subtle nudge of the elbow.

The waitstaff still served complimentary cocktails and hors d'oeuvres. They were needed now more than ever.

"You want anything?" JD asked.

"The usual," I replied.

His attention turned to Sasha.

"A glass of Merlot, if you don't mind. I need something to calm me down."

JD excused himself and made his way to the bar.

Sasha exhaled a breath, trying to let all the stress go. "What a night, huh?"

"At least it wasn't short on excitement," I said.

"That much is true. I wonder if anybody will ever come to another one of my shows after something like this?"

"Maybe it will add to your mystique. A reputation of danger and intrigue."

She smirked. "I like that. I hope you're right."

"I know I'm right. You just gave these people the greatest moment of their life."

Her face wrinkled with confusion. "What do you mean?"

"Now they all have a story to tell about how they escaped death. How they were brave and unwavering in the face of danger. They will tell the story of this evening for the rest of their lives. It will be the subject of their cocktail parties from now on."

Sasha grinned. "I hadn't thought of that. Maybe you're right."

"Trust me. I'm right. I know these people."

"I didn't figure you for running in this circle."

"You'd be surprised at what circles I run in."

Her gorgeous eyes narrowed at me. "Something tells me I shouldn't underestimate you."

I laughed. "I don't mind being the underdog. I like proving people wrong."

JD returned with the adult beverages and passed them out.

Sasha was most grateful. She lifted her glass to toast. "To adventure."

We clinked glasses and sipped our beverages. Her full lips stained the rim of the glass, and she tried to let all the stress and chaos go.

"Let's see if we can't turn this evening around and get you your first sale," I said.

She lifted a curious brow.

"How do you plan on doing that?"

"Well, if you make one sale, another will follow. I suspect there's a high degree of FOMO in this crowd." I glanced around the gallery and looked at the paintings. Her work encompassed a variety of abstract styles. I can't say it was totally my thing, but some of it caught my eye. "Tell you what. I'll buy the brushstroke."

She lifted an astonished eyebrow. "You're serious?"

"Absolutely."

"I thought you hated that painting."

"Let's just say it's growing on me. Who knows? It could skyrocket in value one day. One of the select few paintings that survived the robbery."

She smiled.

"Now, make an announcement that one of your paintings has sold."

Her smile widened. "With pleasure." Sasha grabbed a fork from a tray carried by a passing waitress and tapped the rim of her wine glass. She shouted to the crowd, "I'm pleased to announce that we've made the first sale of the night to Mr. Tyson Wild. Let's give a round of applause for the new owner of Contemplation!"

The crowd was slightly stunned for a moment and didn't know how to respond.

Jack clapped and whistled, and the others followed suit.

Soon, the whole room was cheering. It wasn't long after that when a woman approached Sasha and inquired about another painting.

18

W e stayed at the gallery for the rest of the evening. With a few rounds of drinks, the patrons had put the tumultuous event behind them.

One sale led to another.

Then another.

By the time the liquor ran out, Sasha had sold every painting on offer.

As the evening wound down, she found me in the crowd. Her eyes sparkled with glee. "You were right about that whole *fear of missing out* thing. I can't tell you how many people said they really bonded with their painting. The story of the evening was now part of the history of the artwork, and you were right. It will be a conversation piece at dinner parties across the island. A story for the owner to tell about their acquisition of the fine piece of artwork that now hangs in their living room," she said with a proud smile. Then her face scrunched deep in thought. "Maybe I should orchestrate a robbery at my next event."

I laughed. "I think it would lose its magic if you did it too much."

"Probably right."

"I have to do my due diligence and ask now. You didn't orchestrate this as a publicity stunt, did you?"

She laughed. "No. But I wish I had that kind of marketing savvy."

"It seems like you did okay tonight."

She grinned. "Only because of you. I never sold this much in my life. This is really going to help with rent for the next year or two."

I chuckled. "Good. I'm glad I could be of assistance."

"I feel like I owe you some type of commission. I wouldn't have gotten any of the sales without you."

I shrugged.

"How about you take the painting as my gift?"

"I bought it fair and square."

"I insist. It's the least I could do."

I thought about it for a moment. "Fair enough. But only if you let me take you to dinner as a thank you."

She considered it. "I suppose I could agree to that."

I smiled.

The bar closed, and the party wrapped up.

"I guess I should mix and mingle with some of the guests, but I will deliver your painting tomorrow, and we can discuss dinner plans."

"Sounds like a deal," I said.

"Text me your address."

"What's your number?"

We exchanged digits and said our goodbyes.

JD had been mixing and mingling with the crowd and had found a rich blonde divorcee who seemed quite taken with him.

We left the gallery and met the guys on Oyster Avenue at Red November. We hung out for a few drinks, then had a small gathering on the boat. The usual craziness ensued.

The next morning, I woke with the sunrise and grilled omelets in the galley.

Sasha showed up around 10:30 AM with my painting. She texted me from the parking lot and asked for directions to the boat.

I told her I'd meet her on the dock, then hustled off the *Avventura*.

She unloaded the painting from the back of her Cybertruck. It was wrapped to look like an armored personnel carrier out of a futuristic video game.

She handed me the 36"x 48" canvas. It wasn't that heavy.

"Here you go," she said with a smile as I took the painting from her. Then she handed me a manila folder with a certificate of authenticity. "Are you sure you really want this thing?"

"Absolutely!"

Sasha gave me a doubtful look.

"Who knows? This could be worth a ton of money someday."

"Yeah, long after I'm dead."

"Don't speak negatively over yourself," I said.

"We all gotta die someday."

"All the more reason to live in the moment," I replied.

She smiled. "You know where you're going to put it?"

"I haven't really thought about it." Then an idea popped into my head. "I think I have the perfect place for this. Follow me."

She walked with me as I headed to Diver Down. We pushed inside, and I glanced around.

Teagan gave me a curious look from behind the bar.

I made introductions. "This is Sasha, the artist."

"Nice to meet you, Sasha," Teagan said. "Can I get you anything?"

"No. I'm fine. Thank you."

I moved to a far wall and swapped out a small hanging painting for this one. "For all to enjoy."

Sasha gave a nod of approval.

Harlan sat at the bar, watching the whole thing with a crinkled face. It didn't take a mind reader to see he didn't care much for the painting. But he kept his mouth shut for the time being.

I looked around for another suitable location for the small painting I held in my hand. This would take some thought. I returned to the bar and set it behind the counter for the time being.

"Thanks for bringing that by," I said to Sasha.

"It's my pleasure. And thank you again for last night," she said with a sparkle in her eyes. "Listen, I gotta run. I've got more art to deliver. I'll be in touch," she said in a flirty tone. She addressed Teagan. "It was nice to meet you."

"You as well."

Sasha left the bar and jogged back to her Cybertruck.

"Last night?" Teagan asked with a hint of jealousy.

"Long story."

"I bet."

"Please tell me you didn't pay for that painting," Harlan said.

"Actually, it was a gift. Though I offered to pay."

"Dodged a bullet there," Harlan spoke his mind unfiltered.

"It's modern art," I said.

"It's dog shit. I'm glad you put it over there, so I don't have to look at it."

I laughed. Something told me it wouldn't stay on the wall long.

I regrouped with JD, and we made a game plan for the day. I checked with Denise, and so far, there was no sign of Vernon. I called Paige to see if she had heard anything from him.

19

"No. I'm worried sick," Paige said, panic in her voice. "He's been gone for over 24 hours. What if he's dead somewhere?"

"I'm sure he's okay," I said, without anything to base it on.

"Where would he have spent the night? I called around to all the shelters. They didn't recall seeing anyone who matched his description. Where could he be? What if he wandered off a pier and drowned?"

It was a distinct possibility.

"Let's not go there just yet. I'll have the harbor patrol make a sweep, just to be sure."

"Thank you. I'm just a mess."

"Understandable. Just don't give up hope yet. Has anyone tried to contact you with any demands?"

"Demands?"

"Just thinking outside of the box."

"Who would want to kidnap my grandfather? I don't have any money. I can barely afford his care. He didn't have much savings and hardly any equity in the house. He had taken out a second mortgage to cover some previous health expenses." She broke down into sobs.

I tried my best to comfort her. "We'll check some of his usual haunts today and see if he turns up."

"I appreciate that. Please let me know if you discover anything."

"I will."

I ended the call and filled JD in. We left the *Avventura* and hustled to the parking lot. We hopped into the Porsche, then cruised over to the Reef Shack and talked to the bartender. He hadn't seen Vernon in a long time.

We stopped by the shelters in the area. Nobody recalled seeing Vernon. Paige said she was going to make up some "missing" flyers and hang them at restaurants and bars on Oyster Avenue and at various locations around town.

Afterward, we decided to track down Lamonte's friend Jaxon and see if we could get any information out of him. He wasn't at home, so we headed down to Dowling Street.

I spotted him once again on the corner where Lamonte was shot. He was out slinging dope again. The brilliant Ruby Star Porsche was anything but subtle, and he spotted us a mile away. Jaxon was in the middle of a transaction, leaning against the window of a car at the curb. He took his money and bolted around the corner.

JD gave chase, but this time, he dropped me off a block

before Jaxon's corner. I hopped out and ran up the street while JD continued on and rounded the corner.

Just as he had done the day before, Jaxon barreled up a driveway, ran through the backyard, hopped the fence, and came out on the other side. As he sprinted down the driveway, I was there to greet him.

His eyes rounded when he saw me, and he took off, heading north.

I chased after him, my legs driving forward as fast as I could go.

Jaxon was carrying a little too much weight. He was a big guy, and he was sucking wind. He'd already broken a sweat by this point in time.

I reached him in no time, tackled him to the ground, and used him to cushion the fall.

He grunted and groaned as I crushed him against the ground.

"Coconut County. You're under arrest."

"What the hell for?"

Surprisingly, he didn't put up much of a fight. I wrestled his wrists behind his back and slapped the cuffs on him.

It wasn't long before JD spun around the block and joined me. He parked the Porsche at the curb, hopped out, and called for a patrol unit.

I pulled on a pair of nitrile gloves and carefully dug into Jaxon's pockets. Sometimes, these guys were addicts themselves and would have needles. You needed to be careful, so you didn't get stuck. It was a quick way to end up with something you didn't want.

"Man, I didn't do nothing," he continued to protest. "What the hell are you arresting me for?"

I tossed several baggies of cocaine and heroin onto the ground in front of his face.

"That ain't mine. You planted that."

"All I wanted to do was talk," I said. "You made this difficult."

"What the fuck do you want to talk about?"

"Your buddy Lamonte. I want to know who shot him?"

"Shit, if I knew who shot him, they'd be dead already."

"What about Mario Ruiz?"

"He's high on my list," Jaxon said.

"That's interesting because Mario thinks somebody in your organization killed Lamonte."

Jaxon's face wrinkled. "What the hell are you talking about?"

"He says Lamonte is a snitch."

"Fuck that guy. He's lying. Lamonte ain't no snitch."

"How can you be so certain?"

"I know Lamonte. He's my best friend. I've known him since we were kids. Ruthless Killers for life."

"Tell me about your boss, Anton Lewis?"

"I ain't gotta tell you shit."

"Maybe he thought Lamonte was a snitch and had him whacked?"

"Man, you're out of your damn mind. Mario Ruiz had Lamonte killed because he was hooking up with Esmeralda. Everybody knows that. I told him, keep that shit in your pants. I mean, she's hot. No lie. But that ain't worth getting killed over."

"You know where we can find Anton?"

20

I thought Jaxon was pulling my leg when he told me, but sure enough, we found Anton exactly where Jaxon said he would be.

On the golf course at the country club.

We had commandeered a golf cart from the Pro Shop, and Jack tore down the path to the back nine like a bat out of hell. We were honorary members of the Coconut Key Country Club, and they pretty much gave us the run of the place.

Anton was a walking contradiction.

He wore a white short sleeve polo shirt, exposing his arms that were sleeved in gang tattoos. He wore regulation khaki golf shorts and state-of-the-art golf shoes. High-end professional golf clubs were strapped to the back of his cart.

The other three in his foursome were guys who could have been CEOs, lawyers, or tech moguls.

A cigar hung from Anton's mouth as he teed off on the 16th hole. He drew the clubhead back with ease and made an effortless swing. The driver pinged against the tiny white ball, sending it rocketing down the fairway, landing smack dab in the middle. A short chip to the green, and he could knock it in for birdie.

We hopped out of the cart, and I flashed my badge as we approached the tee box. Anton stepped away to let one of the others in his foursome tee off.

Anton was a tall skinny guy with narrow brown eyes that were red and glassy. He had a trimmed goatee, and the type of dense muscle that those thin, wiry guys have. Deceptively strong.

"What can I do for you, gentlemen?" he asked.

"Need to talk to you about Lamonte Kent."

He frowned and shook his head. "Terrible what happened to him."

"Got any idea who did it?"

"One name comes to mind?"

"That wouldn't happen to be Mario Ruiz, would it?"

He smiled. "You and I are on the same wavelength. It would be a shame if anything were to happen to Mario," he said, trying to maintain an innocent face.

"If you retaliate against Mario, it's going to be rather obvious, don't you think?"

He raised his hands innocently. "I'm not going to do

anything. Fate has a way of dispensing its own brand of justice."

"Mario says he had nothing to do with it."

"Of course, that's what Mario says."

"He says Lamonte was a snitch. He thinks you had him killed."

He scoffed. "That's ridiculous. Lamonte is my boy." Anton paused. "But you tell me... Was he a snitch?"

"There is no record of Lamonte collaborating with law enforcement."

"So Mario is full of shit."

"Where were you yesterday between 10:00 AM and noon?" I asked.

"That's easy. I was right here, working on my handicap."

"What is it?"

"I'm a scratch golfer."

"Impressive. Can anybody verify your whereabouts?"

"I played a round by myself yesterday. But you can check with the Pro Shop. They should have a record of my tee time and my cart rental." He paused. "I really appreciate the thoroughness of your investigation. But Lamonte is like a brother to me. I would never do anything to harm him. And he would never betray me."

"Lamonte had a couple of counterfeit bills in his possession," I said. "Do you know anything about that?"

"Why would I?"

I shrugged.

"Why don't you talk to him about it?"

"I will as soon as he's taking visitors."

"I've been meaning to get by the hospital and see him," he said.

"I'm sure you have," I said with more than a hint of sarcasm.

I gave him a card. "Get in touch if you hear anything. No need to take matters into your own hands. If Mario turns up dead, I'm going to come looking for you."

His face wrinkled. "I don't know why you think I'm so violent. I'm a peaceful man. I'm just out here working on my golf game."

Anton walked away, hopped into the golf cart, and drove off with the others.

"What do you make of that cat?" JD asked.

"I think he runs the show, has his underlings do his bidding, and he never gets his hands dirty."

We hopped in the cart and drove back to the Pro Shop. We decided to have lunch in the mixed grill. JD and I sat outside and watched the golfers come off the 18th green.

I had a bacon cheeseburger with fries, and Jack went with the BLT. I chowed down on the juicy burger that was dripping with grease.

After a few bites, Denise called. "Hey, listen to this."

21

"A woman just called the station," Denise said. "Claims to have seen a man that resembled Vernon at the World War II Museum.

"When?" I asked.

"She just called. Said she's still at the museum. Said Vernon was with a man and a woman."

"Did she give a description?"

"She said the couple was in their mid-30s. They both wore hats, and the woman had short, dark hair. The guy had brown hair." Denise continued. "I told her I would send two deputies over."

"We're on our way," I said.

I ended the call, took another massive bite of my burger, then JD and I hustled out of the grill.

We raced across the parking lot to the Porsche, hopped in, and sped over to the War Museum.

It was a pretty cool place. A step back in time. There was an F4U Corsair and a P-51 Mustang, both polished to perfection. They looked as new as the day they were made.

Canvas webbing hung from the ceiling, and there was an M4 Medium tank that wasn't quite as pristine. Shadow boxes contained full-service uniforms from various branches. There were hundreds of black and white pictures from the war. Display cases were filled with various rifles, dummy hand grenades, and knives. Music from the era pumped through speakers. The place was packed with tourists checking out the historical items.

Dolores waited for us near the entrance. She was in her late 30s with auburn hair, teal eyes, and a narrow face. She was there with her 16-year-old son, Evan.

I showed her a picture of Vernon on my phone. "Are you sure this is the man that you saw?"

She studied the image carefully, then exchanged a look with her son, who also studied Vernon's photograph.

"Yeah, that's him," the boy said.

"You're sure about that?"

He and his mother exchanged another look.

"Yeah, that's him," Dolores said.

I asked her to describe the two people he was with, and she did. But that's where the disagreements came in. Both she and her son gave slightly different accounts of their appearance. Dolores said the guy was 5'10", slightly pudgy, with brown hair, wearing a baseball cap and sunglasses.

"No," her son said. "He was taller, like 6'1". I wouldn't call him pudgy either."

Dolores wrinkled her face at him. "You're getting confused."

"You're the one who's getting confused," Evan said.

"No, I'm not," Dolores replied, growing irritated.

"And you're sure the woman had dark hair," I said.

"Jet black," Dolores replied.

Her son nodded his head in agreement this time.

"I thought it was weird that they kept their sunglasses on inside," Dolores said.

"I've called for a sketch artist," I said. "She's going to meet us here. I want you both to individually give her a description of the people you saw. It doesn't matter if they're different. I want both interpretations."

The sketch artist arrived and spent time with each of them. She drew out a face, then showed it to Dolores for feedback. She made minor adjustments, then repeated the process again until she had representations of both suspects. Then she asked for the son's input and came up with two more sketches.

I examined the final artwork.

The depiction of the woman was relatively similar between Evan's and Dolores's descriptions, but the guy looked completely different.

Evan had described the guy as being tall, with a narrow face and a mustache and goatee. Dolores had described the man as having a slightly pudgy face with no facial hair.

None of the drawings resembled anyone we had met during the course of our investigation.

I gave them both a card, took their information, and thanked them for their cooperation.

The sketch artist texted me all the images, and I texted them to Paris and asked her to broadcast the sketches across the island. Then I sent them to Paige. [Do you recognize these people?]

[No. Should I?]

I told her the story.

[What was Vernon doing at the war museum?]

[Is that someplace he liked to go?]

[I've taken him there a few times, but it's been a while.]

[Does he have any younger friends on the island? Someone he might have visited?]

[No. Most of Vernon's friends are dead, except for the ones in Sunset Palms. And some of those aren't far off.]

[We'll find him]

[Are you sure they really saw him there? Could they be mistaken?]

[Anything is possible. Has anyone made any ransom demands?]

[No. You keep asking that. Do you really think these people kidnapped him?]

[I can't say for sure, but that's a possibility.]

[Why would they take him to the museum?]

[Perhaps to jog his memory.]

[Why?]

I thought for a moment. [Maybe he has information they want.]

[Like what? The meal plan at the Sunset Palms? What information could he possibly have that someone might want?]

[I don't think Vernon has any ID on him. Maybe somebody found him wandering the street, and he's unable to tell them his name or where he lives. Maybe they brought him to the museum to spark things. Mike said Vernon liked to tell war stories.]

[He'd tell stories to anyone who'd listen. But if I found a disoriented old man on the street spouting war stories, I'd probably call the cops if I couldn't get any info out of him. I wouldn't take him to a museum.]

She had a point. I was just grasping at straws.

I told her I'd be in touch, then talked to the woman who ran the ticket booth. She didn't recall seeing Vernon.

"I see so many faces," she said. "They all run together."

I doubted that Vernon bought his own ticket. His two companions had probably arranged entry to the museum.

22

Denise called. "Hey, a patrol unit found a stolen car in a back alley in Jamaica Village. Silver sedan. There was a shell casing in between the passenger seat and the center console. This may be the car used in the drive-by shooting of Lamonte Kent."

"When was the car reported stolen?"

"Day of the shooting."

"Any prints found in the vehicle?"

"The only prints found in the car were matched to the owner, Ted Johnson."

"Text me his information," I said.

"Will do." She gave me a few additional details, then added, "Oh, by the way... I did a little digging on David Chen, the convenience store owner. His son died of a drug overdose last year. I think it's safe to say he has a personal interest in seeing dope dealers removed from the street."

"You think he stole a car, closed the shop, and went vigilante on Lamonte?"

"I know. It's a stretch, but something to consider."

"Indeed." I thanked her and ended the call.

My phone buzzed a few moments later with the info.

JD and I left the museum and headed across the island to find Ted. He lived in the Seaside Vistas on Seabreeze Circle. It was a nice apartment complex with rows of two-story units with teal siding and white trim. There was plenty of open parking, and a few palm trees presided over the complex. But there wasn't an ocean view in sight.

Ted lived in unit #227. We pulled into the parking lot, found a place to park, and hustled up the switchback stairs. I banged on the door to Ted's apartment and shouted, "Coconut County."

Commotion inside filtered down the foyer. Ted pulled open the door a moment later. He was in his early 30s with dark hair, blue eyes, and pale skin. He didn't get out much.

I flashed my badge and made introductions.

"I heard you found my car," he said with hopeful eyes.

"We believe it was used in a drive-by shooting."

He didn't care about that. "Is the car okay?"

"It doesn't appear to be damaged."

He breathed a sigh of relief.

"When was it stolen?"

He shrugged. "I guess sometime during the night. I came out in the morning to go to work, and it was gone."

"Are there any security cameras on the property?"

"Not that I know of."

"When was the last time you saw the vehicle?"

"I guess it was about 8 or 9:00 PM the night before it was stolen. I made a quick trip to the store to get something. I've got an alarm on the car and everything. I don't understand."

"Modern car thieves have gotten pretty sophisticated. They can clone your key fob and get access relatively easily."

"Why bother even locking it up?"

I shrugged.

Criminals had found a way to hack entry and drive systems. Whatever new technology was out, criminals seemed to be two steps ahead.

Ted wasn't really a suspect, but I asked him a few questions anyway. "Where were you yesterday between 10:00 AM and noon?"

"At work."

"Where do you work?"

"I work retail at Shells & Stuff."

"Do you know Lamonte Kent?"

"Who?

"He's the guy that was shot yesterday on Dowling Street. You ever been down there?"

His face wrinkled. "No. I've got no reason to go down there."

"And you don't know the victim socially?"

"I've never heard that name until you just mentioned it."

"No drug use?"

His face twisted again. "No. Do people actually admit to that?"

"Not usually. But users do get nervous when you ask."

"Do I look nervous?"

He didn't strike me as the type of guy who was smoking crack on the weekends, but you couldn't always tell.

I gave him a card and thanked him for his time.

"That's it? When do I get my car back?"

"You'll get a call when the forensic team is finished with it. You'll be able to pick it up from the impound lot."

He frowned. "What am I supposed to do in the meantime?"

"Your insurance company may provide you with a rental. You should notify them of the theft if you haven't already. I'm assuming you've already filled out a police report?"

He nodded.

We left the apartment complex and drove to the hospital to see how Lamonte was doing. He'd been moved to an intermediate care unit and was stable.

The monitor beside his bed blipped with the craggy peaks of his heartbeat. The display read out vital statistics like blood pressure and oxygen saturation. Lamonte was propped up in bed, watching TV. He gave us a curious look as we entered. There was nobody else in the room.

"Who are you?" he asked.

I flashed my badge, and he grimaced.

"I'm Deputy Wild with Coconut County. This is my partner, Jack Donovan."

"What do you want?"

"Well, first, there is the matter of the drugs that were found in your possession. There were enough illegal narcotics to put you away for possession with intent to distribute."

He shook his head. "Man, I don't know nothing about that."

"I'm sure you don't. Maybe you can tell me about the counterfeit hundred-dollar bills that were also found in your possession."

His face wrinkled. "What?"

"I suppose you don't have any idea where those came from, either."

"How the hell should I know? How do you even tell if a bill is counterfeit?"

"There are subtle clues to look for."

"I ain't a bank."

"You sure did have a lot of cash on you."

"What can I say—I like to roll with a bag."

"Tell you what... If you cooperate, help us track down where those counterfeit bills came from, maybe the possession charge goes away."

"You're charging me with possession?"

"Just because you got shot doesn't give you a get out of jail free card."

He didn't like that. Lamonte's face wrinkled with a frown. "What about the guy who shot me? You looking for him?"

"Why don't you tell me who we should be looking for?"

He frowned again. "I don't know."

"You don't know, or you don't want to say?"

"I told you, I don't know," he said, growing angry, then wincing as the tension in his body gave him a sharp reminder of the pain. "I don't remember shit about the last couple of days. All I know is I woke up here with a bunch of holes in me."

"What about Mario Ruiz?"

A guilty frown tugged his face. "I guess maybe he found out."

"That you were hooking up with Esmeralda?"

Lamonte looked confused. "How did you know?"

"It's our job to know."

He responded with a dismissive scowl. "Are you really going to charge me with possession?"

"That's up to you."

"Man, talk to Rafferty. We got a deal."

JD and I exchanged a look.

"What deal do you have with Deputy Rafferty?" I asked.

"I give him information, and he doesn't hassle me."

"So you're a snitch?"

His face wrinkled again. "I ain't no snitch!"

"What do you call it when someone gives information to a police officer?"

He frowned at me. "This is bullshit."

"How long have you had this *deal* with Rafferty?"

"A couple of months."

"And what kind of information do you give him?"

Lamonte shrugged. "You know, tips here and there. What other dealers are doing. Who is moving what. That kind of stuff."

"Who else knows about this deal?"

"Shit, nobody. It better stay that way or my ass is grass."

"Maybe somebody found out."

He frowned again as he thought about it.

"Maybe Anton found out. Maybe he didn't like a snitch in his organization. Maybe he thought you might turn on him someday."

"You think Anton shot me?" he said, his face crinkled with doubt.

I shrugged. "I'm keeping my mind open to all possibilities. You should, too."

Lamonte thought about it for a moment.

"How often do you see Rafferty to give him information?"

Lamonte shrugged. "I don't know. He'll just roll up on me sometimes. Lately, he's been wanting more than information," he said in an annoyed voice.

That piqued my curiosity. JD and I exchanged another glance.

"What do you mean?" I asked.

"It started out as just information. Now he wants money."

"He wants a cut of your sales?"

"He said if I want to stay on the streets, I need to pony up 10%. It's fucking bullshit. That's gotta come out of my end. I gotta kick the money I make up the chain. That shit seriously cuts into my profit margin. I suppose you two assholes are gonna want a cut, too. Is that what this is about? How do you expect a small business to thrive in that kind of environment?"

"I don't know if you classify as a small business."

"I'm an entrepreneur."

I rolled my eyes. "I'm sure you let Rafferty know how displeased you were about his percentage."

"I told him he needed to be careful. Two can play that game."

"What do you mean?"

"I mean, he needs to stay in his lane."

"You threatened a cop?"

"I didn't threaten nobody. But I'm sure that blonde bitch on TV would love to hear about a corrupt cop."

It all came together. I didn't want to think it was possible, but I had that sinking feeling in my stomach. This investigation was going to lead somewhere we didn't want to go.

23

"**A**re you thinking what I'm thinking," JD said.

"I wish I wasn't," I replied.

"I think Rafferty got nervous that the kid was gonna rat him out, or worse."

"So he stole the car, rolled up on the kid, and filled him full of lead?"

"Sounds crazy, doesn't it?"

"Yeah, but it also sounds plausible."

"How do you want to handle this?"

"Turn it over to Internal Affairs," I said.

JD frowned. "Where it will go nowhere."

"Something tells me we're about to get really unpopular around here."

I called the sheriff and updated him on the situation. He responded with a groan. "How solid is your intel on this?"

"It's what the kid says."

"I'd take everything that kid says with a grain of salt. He's a street dealer caught with enough drugs to put him behind bars for 30 years and two counterfeit bills. What do you think he's going to say?"

"You're right," I said. "We should probably just drop this and move on to something else."

Daniels sighed. "Get down to the station. Let's have a little chat with him."

We headed back to the sheriff's department, found Daniels, and waited in his office for Rafferty to arrive.

He'd been working patrol for the county for 15 years and had an unblemished record. In his late 30s now, the patrol car had taken its toll on his form. Lots of doughnuts and fast food made him soft around the midsection. Rafferty had a round face, brown hair, and a mustache. He stepped into the office with a cautious look on his face. "You wanted to see me?"

"Have a seat," the sheriff said, gesturing to a chair across from his desk.

Rafferty stepped inside, closed the door behind him, and the noise from the rest of the office faded away.

Amber rays of sun beamed through the blinds, and motes of dust swirled. The sheriff's desk was stacked with papers. Pictures lined the walls of Sheriff Daniels with various city officials, officers, and a few celebrities. Images of teal water and trophy fish were displayed proudly for the camera.

Rafferty took a seat and gave us a curious look. "What's going on?"

The sheriff sat back and let me take the lead.

"Are you running an off-the-books confidential informant named Lamonte Kent?"

Rafferty's face tightened. "He's just a kid who keeps me in the loop. Tells me what's going on in the neighborhood. I let him do his business and look the other way."

"He was shot yesterday. We just talked to him in the hospital in the intermediate care unit."

Rafferty feigned sympathy. "Sorry to hear that."

"How long have you been working with him?"

Rafferty shrugged. "I don't know. Maybe a few weeks."

"That's not what he says."

Rafferty's face twisted. "I don't give a fuck what he says."

"You don't think this would have been an important detail to note in your reports?"

"Who the hell are you to be asking me these kinds of questions?"

I raised my hands innocently. "No need to get defensive. We're just trying to piece this all together."

"Piece what together?"

I hesitated a moment, then got to the meat of the matter. "Lamonte says you were taking a percentage of his earnings."

"What! That little shit is lying."

I exchanged an ominous glance with the sheriff.

Rafferty's eyes flicked between me and Daniels. "You don't believe that nonsense, do you?"

The sheriff said nothing.

"Lamonte said he threatened to expose you," I said.

"Lamonte is a crack dealer. He will say anything to keep himself from going to jail."

"A stolen silver sedan was found. Forensic investigators recovered a 9mm shell casing. They found a strand of brown hair on the passenger seat."

Rafferty's face wrinkled. "So?"

"We'd like you to provide a DNA sample," I said.

"What, are you guys IA now?"

I shook my head.

"Then get off my back. Whose side are you on, anyway?"

"Just comply with the investigation," Daniels said.

"You can't be serious? You're taking the word of some street punk over mine? You think I stole a car, rolled up on the kid, and shot him because he, what, threatened to expose me? He's making the whole thing up."

"Don't make this difficult," Daniels said.

Fear drenched Rafferty's eyes, and sweat misted his skin. He didn't like being in the hot seat. Nobody did. But he sure wasn't acting like an innocent guy.

Rafferty's concerned eyes flicked between us. It didn't take a rocket scientist to read the room. "If I'm under investigation, I'm going to exercise my right to counsel and deny answering any further questions."

"That's your prerogative," the sheriff said.

"Am I free to go?"

"After you surrender your duty weapon and badge. You're officially on administrative leave, pending the outcome of our investigation."

Rafferty glared at him, then took off his shield and placed his duty weapon on the table along with it. His eyes threw daggers at JD and me as he stormed out of the sheriff's office. He slammed the door, rattling the blinds.

The whole office took note.

"You're not going to make friends around here," the sheriff said after Rafferty left.

"I'm aware."

The gossip was already starting to spread.

My phone buzzed with a call from Paige. I swiped the screen and answered. "What's going on?"

24

"The kidnappers called," Paige said, her voice quivering. "They want $1 million, or they're going to kill him."

She broke down into sobs.

"Just take a deep breath," I said.

"I don't know what I'm going to do. I don't have that kind of money."

"Did you get proof of life?"

"No. I just got off the phone with them."

"How long do you have to get the funds together?"

"They said 24 hours."

"Did they establish a meeting place to make the exchange?"

"No. They said they'd call back with further instructions."

"The next time they call, get proof of life. Did they make any other demands?"

"They told me not to go to the cops. They said they were watching me. And that I should just act normal. What the hell is normal in a situation like this? I'm freaking out. I think *that's* pretty normal."

"Where are you right now?"

"I'm at my apartment."

"Text me your address. I'm going to try to track down that incoming call. Were the kidnappers the last people to call your phone?"

"Yes."

"Okay, hang tight. I'll call you back in a few minutes."

I ended the call and dialed Isabella. I asked her to track the last phone call made to Paige's cell. Her fingers tapped the keys, and a moment later she said, "That's a prepaid cellular. Call was made from the Mega Mart parking lot."

"Can you be more specific?"

"Southeast corner of the lot."

"Where's the phone now?"

"Off the grid."

"Let me know if it pops back up."

"Will do," she said before ending the call.

JD and I hustled out of the station, hopped into the Porsche, and raced over to the Mega Mart. It was one of those big box retailers where you could get everything under the sun for a discount, including groceries. A sea of cars filled the parking lot. There was even overnight camping allowed.

A few security cameras covered the lot.

JD found a place to park, and we hustled inside and found the manager. We made our way to the customer service desk. I flashed my badge and asked to speak with the manager.

The clerk behind the counter got on the intercom and called him to the front of the store. After 15 minutes, he still hadn't arrived. I reminded the clerk that this was, indeed, an emergency.

The clerk didn't seem to care.

The manager finally appeared, but took his time making his way to the customer service desk. He stopped to speak with a checker along the way.

I was pretty irritated by the time he moseyed on up. I displayed my badge again and emphasized the urgency.

"What can I do for you, gentlemen?"

He was in his mid-30s with a bald head and tufts of brown hair on the sides. He wore a blue vest with the Mega Mart logo printed on the chest. He had square glasses and a mustache and wore a light blue button-down and khaki pants. His nameplate read: *Melvin.*

"We believe a kidnapper made a ransom call from the parking lot. We need to take a look at the security footage."

Melvin frowned. "I'm gonna need a warrant for that."

At that point, I wanted to punch the little twerp. But I refrained. "Maybe I wasn't clear. An elderly man was kidnapped. They're threatening to kill him if the ransom demands aren't met."

"So, meet the ransom demands."

My cheeks reddened, and my jaw clenched tight.

JD was about to go off on the guy.

I put a hand on his shoulder to settle him down, preferring to try a more diplomatic approach.

"My hands are tied," the manager said. "All decisions come from corporate. And we value customer privacy here."

"I understand corporate policy. I'm sure you want to help, but what can you do, right?" I said in a sympathetic voice. "I mean, you could be a hero, but corporate is keeping you from getting the recognition you deserve as being an upstanding member of the community. They are keeping you from getting your face on the news, denying you a once-in-a-lifetime opportunity to save someone else's life. I get it. We'll come back with a warrant."

We got a few steps toward the door when he called after us. "Excuse me, deputies. I think I might be able to help you out."

JD and I shared a subtle grin as we walked back to the customer service desk.

The manager slid behind the counter and motioned us to follow. He led us to an office, where he took a seat behind the desk and pulled up the security feed on the monitor. "We have cameras all throughout the store and in the parking lot. What angle do you need to see? Or do you need to see everything?"

I told him we needed to focus on the southeast corner of the lot. With a few keystrokes, he pulled up the footage. We scrubbed through it, looking for anybody in a vehicle that was talking on a phone.

A maroon sedan pulled into the parking lot and found a space a few minutes before the time the call was made to Paige's cell phone. The driver didn't get out of the car. The camera was high on a pole, but we were able to see the driver. He pulled out his cellular device and made a call at the exact moment on the timestamp as when the kidnappers called Paige.

That had to be our guy.

Even though the footage was high-definition, the license plate was a little blurry. I had the manager export the clip and send it to my phone. I texted it to Isabella and asked her to enhance the footage.

I thanked Melvin for his cooperation.

"No problem. Anytime. When do you think this story will break on the news?"

I smiled. "As soon as we track down the perp's license plate, we'll raid his residence and hopefully recover the World War II veteran. You'll be a hero, and I will be sure to let Paris Delaney know that it was all because of you," I said, laying it on thick.

Melvin smiled.

We hustled out of the store and made our way back to the Porsche. By that time, Isabella had texted me the license plate number. She'd already accessed the DMV files and told me that the car was registered to a guy named Ernie Bennett.

We just had one problem.

I couldn't use any of the information that Isabella had given me. And without it, we had no way of proving Ernie made the call. We'd have to subpoena the phone company, but that could take weeks or months for them to comply.

25

I called Denise and asked her to work her magic with the phone company. Sometimes that girl could be quite persuasive. Who knows? Maybe she might get lucky.

JD and I sped across the island to the Lighthouse Landing Apartments. It was a crappy little complex on the northwest side. A single building with teal stucco siding, a flat roof, and a total of eight units that were all serviced by a central staircase with a small courtyard. There was barely enough parking for the residents, and there was no landscaping to speak of.

We parked in the lot of the repair shop across the street, then darted to the complex to do a knock and talk.

Ernie's car was in the parking lot. Isabella had texted me his DMV photo. She had access to just about every database in the world. Nothing was really secure. There were backdoors built into just about every piece of software. And if there wasn't a back door, Isabella could hack her way in.

Ernie's photo somewhat resembled the sketch that Dolores had given to the artist. It wasn't exact, but if you squinted and used your imagination, it was close.

Close enough.

We climbed the steps and found unit #202. I put a heavy fist against the door but didn't announce myself.

Sounds from the TV filtered down the foyer, followed by footsteps. The peephole flickered as Ernie peered through. "Who is it?"

"I got a pizza for #204, but the guy's not home. You want it? It's free."

Ernie unlatched the deadbolt and pulled open the door with hungry eyes that were severely disappointed when he saw that I didn't have a warm pizza box in my hand. His eager expression twisted to confusion. "What the fuck?"

I flashed my badge. "Coconut County. We need to have a word with you."

His eyes rounded, and he tried to shut the door.

I blocked it with my foot, then put a shoulder into it, knocking him back a few feet.

Now, admittedly, this wasn't the proper protocol. But I wasn't playing around. If he had Vernon hostage in his apartment, I was gonna find out. Fortunately, I did smell the odor of marijuana, and that was still illegal. I had reasonable suspicion to believe a crime was in progress once he opened the door.

Ernie was a short guy with a little bit of a belly. He had scraggly brown hair that hung past his ears, a mustache and goatee, and puffy brown eyes. He wore a green patterned short-sleeve button down and cream cargo shorts and sneakers.

He staggered back and scowled at us. "You got no right to enter my home!"

"Where's Vernon?"

He swallowed hard. "What? I don't know what you're talking about?"

He made a move for his waistband.

That was a bad idea.

I didn't know what he had holstered underneath his shirt.

JD and I both drew our pistols. I certainly didn't want to shoot this guy, not after the dubious nature of our entry.

26

"Freeze!" I shouted.

Ernie turned to stone. He raised his hands in the air, eyes wide, trembling with fear. "I was just gonna pull up my pants."

"On the ground. Now. Face down!"

Ernie complied, and JD ratcheted the cuffs around his wrists while I kept my weapon aimed at him.

Once he was secure, JD patted him down but didn't find any weapons. "He's clean," Jack said with a shake of his head.

JD and I took him by the arms and yanked him to his feet. We escorted him into the living room and shoved him onto the couch. There was a tray of weed and a bong. It was all in plain view from the doorway. It would have passed muster if need be.

"Is anybody else in the apartment?" I asked.

Ernie shook his head.

JD stood watch over him while I searched the rest of the one-bedroom apartment. I kicked open the bedroom door and pushed inside, sweeping my barrel across the messy room. The bed was unmade, and clothes were strewn about the floor. Various cups and bottles littered the nightstand by the bed. The place had the dank smell of body odor. I don't think he'd washed his sheets in a year.

I searched the closet and bathroom but didn't find anything. Then, I returned to the living room. "Where's Vernon?"

"Who?"

"Don't play games with me. You made a call from a prepaid cellular demanding a ransom."

Ernie swallowed hard. "No, I didn't."

JD had pulled a cell phone from Ernie's pocket during his initial pat-down. "Want to tell me what this is?"

Ernie swallowed again, then said in a dumb voice, "That's a cell phone."

"That's a prepaid cell phone," I said. "That cell phone made a call to Paige Winslow. We know you're working with an accomplice. Where is Vernon? I want answers. Now! Or things are going to get ugly."

Sweat misted Ernie's skin, and his nervous eyes flicked between the two of us. "I swear to God, I don't know where he is."

"Who does?"

"I don't know."

"Bullshit," JD said.

"I'm telling the truth. I don't have anything to do with it. I was just fooling around."

"Fooling around?" I said in an incredulous tone.

"I had heard about the kidnapping on the news. They interviewed the guy's granddaughter. I found her number online. I thought I'd crank call her."

"You think this is funny?"

"I thought maybe she might pay the ransom," he muttered.

I looked at him in utter disbelief. "What the hell is your problem?"

He shrugged. "I thought it would be some quick cash."

27

J ack called for a patrol unit, and we escorted the perp out of his apartment. A few curious neighbors watched through the blinds as we dragged Ernie across the courtyard.

Jack stuffed him into the back of a patrol car, and we followed to the station. I didn't think Ernie was our guy, but he'd be in the pod for at least a day until his arraignment.

I asked Isabella to do a deep dive into him and see what she could find, then I called Paige and updated her on the situation.

"Are you sure this guy had nothing to do with it?" Paige asked.

"I can't be sure of anything at this point, but I've got my people looking into his background," I said.

"I'm so worried that Vernon's dead somewhere. I know he always talked about not wanting to die in that place. What if he left in the middle of the night and just wanted to go out on his own terms?"

"Don't go there just yet."

"I know. It's just hard. He always said he never wanted to be a burden to anyone."

"Keep your chin up. We'll find him." I told her I'd be in touch and ended the call.

"I don't know about you," JD said, "but I could use a little liquid refreshment right about now."

We left the station and caught happy hour at Flanagan's. It was an old-school pub a few blocks off of Oyster Avenue. Popular with locals and cops. JD and I had been the brunt of curious stares and mutterings of gossip around the station. Instigating the investigation into Rafferty had ruffled more than a few feathers.

Flanagan's smelled like whiskey and beer. JD and I took a seat at the bar and ordered a round. There were a few cops from the department working their way through a pitcher. Our presence drew annoyed eyes. I suspected JD had chosen this location on purpose to see just how bad the sentiment was.

It didn't take long for Rexford to approach. He was a big, barrel-chested guy with a head so slick it looked like it was polished with wax. He had a thick reddish brown mustache and hairy arms. He ambled around the bar and leaned on the counter next to JD and me. "What's with this investigation into Rafferty?"

I shrugged. "There are allegations that Rafferty is on the

take. It was brought to the sheriff's attention, and IA is handling it."

"You brought it to the sheriff's attention," he said with narrow eyes, staring me down.

"What was I supposed to do?"

"Just because some street thug makes an allegation doesn't mean it's true."

"Agreed. I'm sure IA will get to the bottom of it."

Rexford didn't like that answer. "So Rafferty's reputation and career get ruined in the meantime?"

"One dirty cop makes us all look bad."

Rexford scoffed. "You two aren't even real cops. What do you do anyway? You run around, have a good time, raise hell. You two break your fair share of rules. Maybe you ought to get investigated."

"I know you're close with Rafferty. I know these kinds of allegations are upsetting."

"Upsetting? How about infuriating? It seems anybody can say anything these days and ruin a man's life."

"Like I said, I'm certain IA will get to the bottom of it." I wasn't certain of anything. I was willing to bet money it would get swept under the rug.

Rexford's cheeks reddened. He looked like he wasn't too far away from throwing a punch. I was ready for anything, but the last thing I needed was to get into a fight with another cop in this bar.

"Watch your back, Wild. 'Cause nobody else is going to." His eyes flicked to JD. "That goes for your lapdog, too."

JD got off his bar stool, and I had to hold him back.

Jack made an obscene gesture. "I got your lapdog right here, bitch."

28

"Hey! Take it outside," the bartender yelled, sensing the impending brawl.

Rexford stared us down for another moment, then backed away and rejoined his friends.

"Better walk away, punk ass," JD muttered as he took his seat.

The bartender joined us and leaned against the counter. "Once you finish your drinks—on the house—why don't you go somewhere else?"

JD's face twisted with a scowl. "Are you kicking us out?"

"I'm asking you nicely to find some other place to enjoy your evening. I can tell where this is going. Trust me, you'll thank me in the morning."

JD frowned and shot a few angry looks down the bar at Rexford and company.

"Let's get out of here," I muttered.

We both slugged down our whiskey and left the bar.

We hit the sidewalk and strolled up to Oyster Avenue.

Jack grumbled the whole way. "I should have laid that asshole out."

"I think that's just what he was looking for. He wants an excuse to get us in hot water."

"Shit, he's probably just as corrupt as Rafferty."

Across the street, a woman with raven hair was tagging the side of the building with spray paint. Her long locks were pulled back into a ponytail, and she wore a ball cap backward and a respirator.

You either had to be incredibly stupid to tag a building directly across from Flanagan's, knowing the number of cops that frequented the place, or you were trying to make a statement. I think this girl was making a statement. Bold and unapologetic.

She clearly didn't like the mayor.

This was the graffiti artist we were looking for.

She was putting the finishing touches on an image of the mayor stealing money from someone's pocket.

JD was still too preoccupied with Rexford to notice. I nudged him and pointed out the artist. "Should we arrest her?"

He looked at the artwork for a second. "Well, she's not lying."

We waited for the traffic to clear, then hustled across the street just as the artist applied the last stroke. She stood up, stepped back, and marveled at her work for a moment.

"Excuse me," I said, flashing my badge as I approached.

Her eyes rounded when she saw me, and she wasn't about to stick around to make introductions. She spun around and took off toward Oyster Avenue. She bolted around the corner, weaving through the crowd of tourists that drifted up and down the boulevard.

I gave chase, but I didn't put a lot of effort into it—not because of my feelings about the mayor, but because I recognized those eyes. They were unmistakable.

I rounded the corner, and the raven haired artist zigged and zagged through the crowd then darted into the street.

Horns honked, and tires squealed, but she made it to the other side, barreled through a few more pedestrians, then darted into an alley.

I let her go and waited for JD to catch up with me.

"Was that who I think it was?" JD asked.

I nodded.

"Well, that's interesting," he said, amused.

We headed up to the Oasis Lounge to continue our happy hour in a more casual environment. Walls of flat-panel screens displayed images of white sand beaches and sapphire waves. Palm trees fluttered in the breeze. It was like stepping into a virtual resort. Stunning beauties pranced around in skimpy attire, rivaling the scenic beauty on the monitors.

JD and I grabbed a seat at a cocktail table with plush chairs and sat back and enjoyed the scenery. It wasn't long before a waitress dropped by the table to take our order.

She returned in short order and delivered the glasses of amber goodness.

Chill music pumped through speakers, but it wasn't so loud that you couldn't have a conversation. I gave it a few minutes, then called Sasha.

It rang a few times, then went straight to voicemail.

It didn't surprise me that she didn't pick up. She was probably still out of breath and panicked from running from the scene of the crime. I think I liked her graffiti more than I liked her abstract work. I left a message. "We are at the Oasis Lounge. I thought you might like to join us for a drink. And for what it's worth, I think the mayor is a scumbag, too."

I ended the call and slipped the phone back into my pocket. The cards were on the table. It would be interesting to see how she played it from here.

29

I was more than a little surprised to see Sasha strut into the Oasis Lounge. JD and I had stuck around for a few drinks and were just about to move on.

Sasha set the place on fire.

She had dolled herself up in a skimpy little black cocktail dress that hugged her petite form and sparked impure thoughts. The dress had a deep V neckline and an exposed back that showed off her toned body and smooth skin. Strappy heels accented her long legs, and she drew plenty of lustful stares from the sharks in the crowd. Her gorgeous eyes scanned the club, and I waved her over.

She had guts. I had to give her that.

She strutted across the bar, breaking hearts as she moved. Sasha joined us at the table. "Is this seat taken?"

"Be my guest," I said, standing up to greet her.

She plopped into the seat and sat with poise and confidence. "So, anything exciting happening in your world?"

I had tipped my hand, but she was still playing it cool.

"Oh, the usual. Working a potential kidnapping case, chasing down counterfeiters."

Sasha lifted a curious brow. "Counterfeiters. That sounds interesting. Any leads?"

"Nothing yet."

"Isn't that a bit out of your jurisdiction? That comes under the purview of the Treasury Department, doesn't it?"

"Yes, but we're part of a joint task force, or so it would seem."

"Never a dull moment."

"Never," JD said with a grin.

"What about you? How's your day?"

"Good. Sold a few more paintings. I can't complain."

"Create any new artwork?" I said with a slight smirk.

"I'm always creating," she said.

I held out my hand, and she took it.

There were still speckles of spray paint on her fingertips and nails. When she saw that I noticed, she pulled her hand away.

"I was working on another piece in the studio," she said.

I gave her a doubtful look. "We both know you weren't working in the studio."

She took a deep breath and owned it. "So, are you going to arrest me?"

I exchanged a look with JD. "We didn't really get a good look at the vandal. I couldn't swear to her identity in a court of law."

Sasha seemed relieved. "Vandal?"

"How would you describe it?"

"Describe what?" she asked coyly.

"Someone who defaces private property."

"I don't know if I would call it defacing. It could be considered an improvement. Perhaps an awareness campaign."

"You know, I'm running for mayor," Jack said.

Sasha lifted an intrigued eyebrow.

"I could use a campaign logo."

"I only get involved with causes I believe in. What's your platform?"

"Half the city is on the take," JD said. "My platform is to clean that up."

"Does that mean getting rid of all the graffiti artists?"

He sneered at her playfully.

"I can think of one that absolutely needs to be punished," I said.

"That sounds naughty. Maybe I should get in trouble more often," she said with a flirty gaze.

"I think maybe you should lay off the graffiti work," I said.

She frowned at me. "Somebody's gotta get the message out. Do you want four more years of this nonsense?"

"If I get elected," JD said, "I can promise you it's gonna be four years of good times."

"You need a slogan. Something inspiring. Uplifting. Aspirational."

"I agree. What do you have in mind?"

"I'm an artist, not a copywriter. Certainly not a marketing genius, or I'd be rich by now."

"After that gallery showing, you might be well on your way," I said.

She smiled. "At least I'm not wondering where rent is going to come from next month."

She thought about it for a moment. "Rock solid leadership, restoring trust."

JD considered it. "I like that. It plays off Wild Fury. It needs a little something, though."

"It's a work in progress," Sasha said. "Feel free to adapt and improvise."

"Does this mean you're in?"

"I guess I could try to come up with a few designs. That is, of course, if I'm not in jail. Her flirty eyes flicked to me."

"Like I said, I can't be sure who I saw defacing that wall."

Sasha smirked.

JD's phone buzzed with a text. His face glowed from the display as he read the message. After a brief exchange, he grinned and slipped the phone back into his pocket. "If you'll excuse me, opportunities await."

I had no doubt he had lined up something in a petite little package.

We said our goodbyes, and JD slipped out of the club.

"He's quite the character, isn't he?" Sasha said.

"One-of-a-kind," I replied.

"I don't know you guys well, but from what I do know, I think he'll probably make a good mayor."

I laughed. "You might be right. It would definitely be different."

Sasha took another sip of her drink. "So, about this punishment. What exactly did you have in mind?" she asked with a naughty glimmer in her eyes.

30

We caught a cab back to the *Avventura*, and the driver couldn't go fast enough. Sasha had definitely lit the embers of desire. She grabbed my hand and placed it on her sumptuous thigh, then guided it up to the hemline of her skirt. I didn't need any guidance after that point. I knew exactly what to do.

The cab driver was no rookie. He'd had tipsy, lustful couples in the back of his car on numerous occasions. I think he read the room pretty well. His eyes kept flicking to the rearview mirror, hoping to catch glimpses of the lurid show. I don't think he could see exactly where I had my hand, but it didn't take a rocket scientist to figure it out, especially with Sasha's subtle whimpers and moans, which she tried to hide but failed to do.

We finally turned into the parking lot of Diver Down, and the driver pulled around by the dock. I think he was sorry to see us get out of his car. I threw a few bills at him, and we hopped out of the vehicle.

Sasha giggled as she adjusted her skirt. I took her hand and escorted her down the dock to the boat. She'd never seen the superyacht before and was quite impressed.

"This is not exactly what I was expecting."

"What, were you hoping for something bigger?"

"I think this is big enough."

I escorted her across the passerelle to the aft deck. Buddy went ape-shit at the salon door, barking and wagging his tail.

I slid open the glass doors and kept him from jumping all over Sasha. She knelt down and loved on him, and the little Jack Russell ate it up. Pretty soon, he was licking her face.

"Easy there, boy. That's my job."

Sasha stood up, and her gorgeous eyes sparkled with desire. "Well, get to work."

She didn't have to tell me twice.

We stepped into the salon, and I slid the door shut. As soon as I did, we were locked at the lips. They were soft and luscious, and I didn't mind kissing them at all.

We were all over each other—hands groping and fondling, peeling off items of clothing. Within a couple steps, we were both partially disrobed. A few more steps and her dress was on the deck. We left a trail of garments behind us and took advantage of all that the sofa had to offer.

And it offered quite a lot.

We went for broke, our hips colliding, our bodies undu-lating in rhythmic motion. Breathy moans of ecstasy filled the salon. Not to be outdone, Buddy chimed in with howls of his own.

31

When we'd worn ourselves out, we caressed each other on the couch, our bodies slick and glistening with sweat, heartbeats pounding.

"Is this how you interrogate all potential suspects?"

"Not all. Only the pretty ones."

She smiled.

"But you better lay off the graffiti."

"What graffiti?" she said in a diabolically innocent voice.

"Surely you can put your talents to better uses."

"And what uses would those be?"

"I can think of a few areas where your skill would be best applied."

"Can you?" she said coyly.

I nodded.

"Well, that was just a warm-up. We're just getting started."

I liked the sound of that.

She planted her full lips on mine and did a good job of inspiring round two.

Afterward, we decided it was probably best if we gathered our belongings and made our way up to my stateroom. There was no telling who JD would come back to the boat with. He could have a companion or two, or an entire entourage.

We climbed into bed, and Sasha nuzzled close. I could think of worse ways to spend an evening.

I never heard JD return to the boat. He must have found other accommodations for the evening.

In the morning, Sasha and I tumbled around the sheets before getting up for breakfast. I grilled a nice spread in the galley, and we enjoyed a relaxing meal on the sky deck as amber rays cascaded across the marina.

"You guys are really living the life," she said.

"We try."

"One of these days, I'm gonna have yacht money. Tell me again, how can you afford all this?"

I gave her an abbreviated version of the story.

I'm not sure she bought it.

"I have no doubt you'll accomplish anything you put your mind to," I said.

She smiled with pride. "Thank you."

"You seem dedicated and a hard worker."

"You've never seen me work."

"Well, I've seen you put in a good deal of effort," I said with a smirk.

"Like I said, we're just warming up."

"If that was a warm-up, I'm looking forward to the next time we get together."

"So, you think there's going to be a next time?"

"I'm not going to complain if there is."

"Good." She smiled.

My phone buzzed with a call from Paige. I swiped the screen and held the phone to my ear. "Good morning. I hope everything's alright."

"No. It's not alright. I mean, I guess it's better than the alternative. But, it's not good. I just got a call from the real kidnappers."

"How do you know?" I replied.

"Because they provided proof of life. They've got Vernon," she said, breaking down into sobs.

"At least we know he's alive. I need you to send me whatever they sent you."

"They didn't send me anything. They put him on the phone. I talked to him."

"What did he say? Is he okay?"

"He says he's having a blast."

My face wrinkled. "What do you mean?"

"He says he's having a great time. They took him to the museum. They took him fishing. They're treating him well. Halfway through the conversation, he didn't even know who I was."

"What do they want?"

"They say they want war bonds. I don't know what they're talking about. Vernon doesn't have any war bonds."

My brow knitted as I thought about it. "Are you sure he doesn't have any stashed anywhere?"

"I guess it's possible. I put most of his stuff in storage when I moved him into the assisted living facility. I've got a few things in my apartment, but I've never seen any war bonds. I mean, I guess there could be some in one of the boxes at the storage facility." She thought about it for a second. "You know, he was always telling these crazy stories about the war. He kept talking about this covert mission. I always thought it was BS, especially in recent years. The stories got more and more extravagant."

"Tell me about this covert mission," I said.

32

"Vernon said that he was on this top secret mission transporting war bonds to Panama," Paige said. "The base had been built in 1918. During the war, it was used as a submarine base, and the war bonds were used as an off-the-books payment to some of the Panamanian officials to grease the wheels during the expansion. At this point in time, the outcome of the war was uncertain at best. Vernon said that they were traveling on a merchant ship when it was sunk by a U-boat in the Caribbean. Vernon and another crew member survived. They were the only two. Since the whole thing was off-the-books, there was no record of it, and nobody went looking for the war bonds." She paused. "It all sounded a little fantastical to me. But according to Vernon, there were thousands and thousands of war bonds sealed in a chest. If it's true, they're all at the bottom of the ocean in the wreckage. He said the face value on those bonds was $10,000 apiece."

"If I recall, those things paid interest up until the '80s," I said.

"Are they still worth anything?"

"Absolutely. But most of them have been redeemed by now."

"So, there could be millions of dollars down there."

"Could be," I said. "Do you have any idea where this ship went down?"

"No. But Vernon said he made a map."

"What happened to his shipmate?" I asked.

"I think he died in the late '80s. Vernon said they always talked about going out there and trying to find the ship, but they never got around to it. You think if there was that much money at stake, they would have at least made an effort. But Vernon never was a scuba diver." Paige paused. "I never gave the story any merit, but do you think those war bonds could still be down there? Is that really why they kidnapped him?"

"You said Vernon loved to tell stories about the war. Maybe somebody overheard him, and that put an idea in their head."

"He could have told the story to anybody," she said.

It was all starting to make sense. "I can think of a few obvious suspects. I'll get my people on this, and I will call you back. Let me know if you hear anything else from the kidnappers."

"Okay," she said in a frightened voice.

I ended the call, then texted Isabella. I asked her to track the last incoming call to Paige's phone and to dig into this covert story of Vernon's to see if there was any merit to it.

Sasha had listened to the entire conversation. "Kidnappers?"

I nodded.

"Sounds serious."

"It is."

"There goes my idea of spending the day together."

"Sorry, duty calls."

Sasha and I took our plates down to the galley and cleaned up.

"I think I'm going to sneak out of here and let you take care of business."

"I can give you a ride back to your place."

"Are you sure it's no trouble?"

"No trouble at all."

I called JD and filled him in on the situation, then grabbed the keys to the Devastator and escorted Sasha to the parking lot. I drove the Plum Crazy Purple 1970 Barracuda across the island to her apartment.

"You can just drop me off here," she said as I pulled around to the main entrance. She leaned across the console and planted her plump lips on my cheek. "I had fun last night."

"So did I."

"I hope you catch your bad guys and get Vernon back."

"Me too," I said.

She hopped out of the muscle car and darted into the lobby.

I drove back to the marina, and Isabella called me along the way. "The call to Paige's cell phone was made from the payphone at the gas station near the Pussycat Palace."

I knew from experience there were no cameras that caught an angle on the payphones. They were on the side of the building, obscured from the view of the cashier. There weren't many payphones left on the island, but there were a few. Some in hotels, some in restaurants near the restrooms, a few at the bus terminal, and one at the mall. I'm sure there were others.

"What about his covert mission?" I said.

"I can't find anything about it. If it's true, it must have been totally off-the-books and never made it into the database. I can tell you this... The Treasury Department keeps a record of every bond issued. There is a slew of consecutive serial numbers that were issued during the war that have never been redeemed."

That piqued my curiosity. "How much are we talking about?"

"Series E bonds were sold beginning in 1941, initially with a 10-year maturity date, later extended, and continued to accrue interest for up to 30 or 40 years. The last Series E bond was issued in 1980. With a face value of $10,000 per bond, plus interest, I'd say you're looking at around $23,575.52 per bond, off the top of my head."

"Off the top of your head," I teased.

"How many bonds are we talking about?"

"10,000," I said.

"That's 235 million and change."

That hung there for a moment.

"That's a lot of money," I said. "The only problem is those bonds were non-transferable. They were registered securities."

"This is a highly unusual situation," Isabella said. "But it's possible some kind of a deal was made. Perhaps they were issued blank and the serial numbers marked. These things can be redeemed at any bank, but I'm sure walking into your local branch with 10,000 of them is going to raise a few eyebrows." Then she added, "Those bonds would also have significant value on the collector market. Somebody would pay a boatload for those. Either way, they're valuable. If they exist."

33

JD and I headed back to the Sunset Palms. We pushed inside, and I greeted the receptionist at the front desk with a smile. I asked if Mike was on shift. She said he was and called him to the front desk.

He showed up a few moments later with a concerned look on his face. "I hope you're here with good news."

"Not exactly," I said. "Vernon's been kidnapped."

His brow lifted with surprise. "Have they made any ransom demands?"

"They have."

"Do you have any idea who's responsible?"

"You mentioned Vernon had a lot of war stories to tell."

He nodded.

"Did he ever talk to you about any war bonds?"

Mike thought about it for a moment. "Not that I recall."

"No talk of a covert mission?"

"No. Why?"

I had my suspicions about Mike. He had access to Vernon. Probably heard every story that Vernon had to tell. Twice.

"Did anybody else have regular access to Vernon?"

He shrugged. "Just the staff. His granddaughter. The other residents."

"Did he have any other visitors?"

"Not that I recall, but you can check the logs. They're pretty accurate. We require all visitors to register when they enter the facility." Then he added, "But, I can't say who he told what on his excursions outside the facility."

"How often did he sneak off the grounds?"

"A couple times a month, maybe."

I thanked him for his time, then we talked to a few other staff members before leaving. Nobody admitted to hearing anything about the war bonds or the covert mission.

"What do you make of Mike?" JD asked as we strolled through the parking lot toward the Porsche.

"He certainly had access to Vernon." I pulled up the sketches that our artist had drawn of the suspects at the War Museum.

"You know, if you kind of blend those two images together, there are some similar features to Mike," JD said.

I called Isabella and asked her to run background on Mike and look at his cellular history.

"If he does have Vernon, where is he keeping him?" JD asked.

"I say we stop by his residence and look around."

I called the sheriff and asked him to put surveillance on Mike while we snooped around.

"I'll put Erickson and Faulkner on it," he said. "They're not going to like it, and you guys aren't winning any popularity contests lately."

"I'm not in this for the popularity."

"That's abundantly clear."

The sheriff connected me with Denise, and she looked up Mike's address. He lived in the Windwood Apartments on Pearl Street.

JD and I swung by and found a place to park. We hopped out and strolled the pathway to his unit. It was a nice complex with a series of freestanding buildings, eight units each—four up, four down. Towering palms swayed overhead, and the central focal piece of the complex was a crystal clear pool with a barbecue grill and several lounge chairs. The parking lot was open and not secured. Anybody could go on the grounds.

We found his building and climbed the steps. I banged on the door to unit B201, not expecting a reply. I put my ear to the door and listened for any sounds.

There was a TV on inside, but I didn't hear anything else.

I banged on the neighbor's door, and a young blonde in her 20s answered after I identified myself. She pulled open the door and looked at us with doubtful eyes. "Are you two really cops?"

I let her have a closer look at my badge for good measure.

"Have you seen anything unusual next door?"

"What do you mean, unusual?"

I showed her a picture of Vernon. "Have you seen him come or go from the apartment?"

She studied the image for a moment. "No."

"You're sure?"

"I mean, I haven't been spying on my neighbor, but the only person I've seen go in or out of that apartment is the guy who lives there. I don't think I even know his name."

"Mike."

Recognition flashed in her eyes. "Yeah, that's it." Then she added, "His girlfriend comes over now and then, but not a lot." Her face crinkled as she thought. "Actually, I don't think he's here much. He must stay at her place."

"Who's his girlfriend?"

She shrugged. "She's cute-ish. Kinda heavy."

Compared to this girl, everybody looked heavy.

"Can you describe her?" I asked.

She shifted onto one hip and scrunched her lips. "It's been a long time since I've seen her. They could have broken up. But I think she had shoulder-length brown hair. Blue eyes. Pretty face."

I gave her my card. "If you happen to see Vernon in the area, give me a call."

She smiled. "Will do."

We climbed down the steps, and I banged on the downstairs neighbors' doors, but nobody answered.

We walked around to the back of the building and looked onto the balcony. The blinds were closed, and I couldn't see into the apartment.

I didn't think Vernon was here.

Isabella called as we walked back to the parking lot. "I looked into Mike. No criminal history. Judging by his phone records, he goes to work, to his apartment, and he spends a lot of time at another residence, which I assume is his girlfriend Monica Presley's. She also works at Sunset Palms."

"We've met her before."

"I did some digging into her as well. No criminal history. I'll keep digging."

I thanked her and ended the call.

JD and I climbed into the Porsche and headed across the island to pay Monica a visit at home.

34

I banged on the door at Monica's several times, but nobody answered. JD and I took the opportunity to walk around the property, peering and through windows.

Neither of us saw anything unusual.

JD muttered, "Want to break in and take a look around?"

I looked at him like he was crazy. "No. I do not want to break in."

Jack frowned and shrugged.

We left the property and started knocking on neighboring doors, asking if anyone had seen an old man coming or going from the property.

Nobody recalled seeing Vernon.

Monica pulled into her driveway just as we were walking back toward the Porsche. JD and I hustled across the street and confronted her as she stepped out of her red compact SUV. It was a Toyoma Sport-4.

I flashed my badge to jog her memory, even though we had already met.

She looked flustered. "You startled me."

"Sorry about that. I just need to ask a few additional questions."

"Certainly. Do you mind if I get my groceries in?"

"Not at all. Let us give you a hand with that."

She popped the back hatch, and we grabbed handfuls of plastic bags and helped her carry the groceries inside. She had the usual items—milk, bacon, eggs, frozen vegetables, frozen pizza, burritos, and other microwavable items.

She unlocked the door, and we followed her inside, down the foyer, and into the kitchen.

JD and I both took in the surroundings, looking for any sign of Vernon.

"Just set those on the counter," she said.

We did, then went back for another round and made short work of it.

Once we were inside, JD asked to use the restroom. Monica pointed him in the right direction, and I kept her occupied in the kitchen.

"Any word on Vernon?"

I told her about the kidnapping.

She reacted with surprise and concern. With round eyes, she gasped. "I hope he's okay. He's quite a handful to take care of. I wonder if he's getting his medications and everything he needs."

"He sounded good when Paige talked to him."

She exhaled with relief. "That's encouraging. Do you have any leads?"

"That's why we want to talk to you," I said.

That hung there for a moment.

"I'm not sure how I can help. I've already told you everything I know."

"We believe the kidnappers have some connection to Vernon."

"You mean, you think it's someone he knows?"

I nodded. "Someone who would have detailed knowledge of his war stories."

"He had quite a few of those," she admitted.

"Did he ever tell you about a covert mission involving war bonds?"

She shrugged it off. "Oh, I don't know. He told me so many things, and I wasn't sure how much of it to believe. If you listen to Vernon, he was the greatest war hero of all time." Then she added, "Not to diminish his service in any way, mind you. I think everyone who serves is a hero. But sometimes, to listen to him talk, he single-handedly brought down the German army."

"He was in the Navy."

"You get my point."

I chuckled. "Can you think of any other visitors he may have had over the last several months that he would have confided in?"

"Just his granddaughter. I guess, the staff members." Her face wrinkled. "But you don't really suspect staff involvement, do you?"

"We're not ruling anything out at this point," I said.

She nodded and swallowed. I had to admit, she looked a little nervous.

"If I'm not being too personal, are you seeing Mike?"

She nodded. "How did you know? Did he say something?"

"No," I said, pointing to a picture of the couple on the side of the refrigerator.

She laughed, expelling nervous energy. "Oh, I see. You *are* a detective."

"How long have you two been together?"

She sighed and looked to the ceiling as she thought about it. "I guess about a year now."

"I guess it's going well?"

She smiled. "I think this one could stick. But if he doesn't make it official pretty soon, I'm going to start nudging him in that direction."

"Well, I hope he recognizes what he has," I said.

She blushed and batted her lashes.

JD rejoined us in the kitchen and gave me a subtle head shake. He'd snuck off, looking through the house, and hadn't seen any sign of Vernon.

I thanked Monica for her time, and she walked us to the door.

"Thanks for helping with the groceries," she said.

"Our pleasure," JD replied.

We stepped onto the porch and walked back toward the Porsche. Monica hovered in the doorway for a moment to watch us go, then closed and latched the door.

Jack muttered, "Where do you think they're keeping him?"

"They *are* acting a little funny, but it doesn't mean they kidnapped Vernon," I said as we hopped into the car. I called the sheriff. "I need more surveillance. Put another team on Monica Presley."

"Oh, sure. I'm not short-staffed or anything," he said.

"Well, I guess we could let our best lead slip away."

"Or maybe you two numbskulls could sit on her."

"We've got other leads to run down," I said.

"Like what?"

My phone buzzed with a call from an unknown number. I recognized the prefix.

"I'm gonna have to call you back," I said. "I gotta take this."

He grumbled something as I ended the call and answered the other line.

"Is this Deputy Wild?"

"Speaking."

"This is Lamonte. I remembered who gave me the hundred-dollar bills."

"Who?"

"If you want to know, then we need to work out a deal."

I knew that was coming. "What kind of deal?"

"All charges against me get dropped. I'll help you track down the counterfeiters, and we forget about the drug possession."

"I'm sure we can work something out. I'll talk to the prosecutor."

"In writing. I want a deal in writing."

35

The Treasury Department and the Assistant US Attorney wanted the counterfeiters a lot more than they wanted Lamonte. I had a written deal in no time. JD and I returned to the hospital to get the information from Lamonte. I handed him the formal agreement, and he looked over it.

Agent Foster joined us.

"Satisfied?" I asked.

"Just so we're clear, nothing I tell you can be used against me, right?"

"Short of murder, you're off the hook," I said. "Going forward, if you break the law, you will be prosecuted."

He didn't like that idea. "You mean you can't give me a pass to keep dealing on the street? I can keep you supplied with information."

"The deal you had with Rafferty no longer exists. This is the new deal. Take it or leave it," I said.

He frowned, then said, "I got them from a regular client of mine. Nolan. He bought some coke and paid for it with the hundreds."

JD and I exchanged a look.

"Describe Nolan," I said.

"Thin. Shaggy brown hair. Dark eyes. Narrow face. Mid-20s."

It sounded a lot like Sasha's friend from art school.

"And he paid you with the counterfeit bills the day you were shot?"

Lamonte nodded.

"If you're lying to me..."

"I ain't lying. I swear."

I muttered to JD, "What's Nolan's last name?"

He thought about it for a moment. Sasha had mentioned it when she introduced him at the gallery.

"Maxwell," JD replied.

"You know the guy?" Foster said.

"I think so." I called Denise and had her look up his information.

She texted me his address and his DMV photo. I showed the image on my phone to Lamonte. "Is this the guy?"

"Yeah, that's him."

"You're sure about that?"

"Positive. I've been selling him drugs for a couple years now."

"Thank you. You've been helpful."

We stepped out of the room and had a conference with Foster.

"How do you know he's not making up some bullshit story to save his ass?"

I shrugged. "We don't."

"How well do you know this Nolan guy?"

I shook my head. "Just met him."

"Let's go talk to him."

"Why don't you let us handle this?"

She lifted a stunned eyebrow. "Excuse me? Why would I do that?"

"Because you look like you want to kill someone right now. I think this requires a more subtle approach."

"Um, in case you forgot, my partner was killed. I want everyone involved with Nevsky to go down. Besides, I'm way cuter than either of you. Nolan will want to talk to me."

She strutted down the hallway toward the elevators.

JD and I exchanged a shrug, then followed.

Foster pressed the call button. We caught up and waited for the elevator to arrive.

The door slid open, and we stepped aboard and plunged down to the lobby. We hustled outside to the Porsche and zipped across the island to the Bayshore Apartments.

Foster followed.

The place wasn't much to speak of. A drab complex with flamingo pink stucco walls and white trim. The building had a U shape, and there was a central courtyard with a staircase that led up to the second floor. The siding was grungy and grimy, and the grass was a little overgrown. A few withering palm trees presided out front. There was no security, no covered parking. I figured Nolan was doing the whole *starving artist* thing.

We parked in the lot, strolled through the courtyard, and climbed the steps. I banged on unit #206.

There was no answer.

I knocked again and waited another few minutes.

Finally, signs of life emanated from within. Footsteps shuffled to the door, and the peephole flickered as Nolan peered through. He pulled open the door and wiped the sleep from his eyes. I gathered Nolan wasn't much of a morning person.

"What's going on?"

I flashed my badge for good measure and reminded him where we met.

"I remember. What can I do for you?"

"You know Lamonte Kent?"

He shook his head. "No. Never heard of him."

"Really?" I showed him a picture of Lamonte on my phone. "Ring any bells?"

His eyes flashed with recognition. "Yeah, I've seen him around."

"A couple days ago, you made a purchase from Lamonte with two counterfeit $100 bills," Foster said.

His brow lifted with surprise. "What!?"

"I don't care that you used the money to buy cocaine. I want to know where the bills came from."

Nolan stammered, "I don't know anything about counterfeit money. That could have come from anywhere."

"Where do you think it came from?" Foster asked in a condescending tone.

He shrugged. "I don't know."

Nolan didn't have two nickels to rub together. I'm pretty sure he'd remember where he got two $100 bills.

"Oh, wait," he said, pretending to remember. "I sold a guitar last week. The guy paid me in cash."

"What's his name?"

"Shit, I don't remember?"

"How did you meet this guy?"

He hesitated for a moment. "I was at the guitar shop, and I saw this guy playing a guitar exactly like mine. I told him he could buy mine for half price. It was in mint condition. I told him to stick around, and I'd come back with the guitar. We met in the parking lot and did the deal."

I wasn't sold. "You happen to catch his name?"

"Ben. Brad. Something like that."

"And you're sure that's where the bills came from?"

"Yeah, absolutely," Nolan said.

"You mind if we take a look around your apartment?"

36

Nolan's face wrinkled. "What are you looking for? More counterfeit bills?"

"Something like that," I said.

"I don't think I have any more around," Nolan said, "but feel free to look."

He stepped aside and let us into the apartment. I was surprised that he agreed.

We entered the small one-bedroom and looked around. In the living room, there was a flatscreen display, a gaming console, large speakers, a leather sofa, and a glass coffee table. There were a few plants in the corners. The way the unit was laid out, there was no balcony and no exterior windows, except in the far bedroom. It had an open floor plan from the living room to the kitchen. Cheap laminate countertops and crappy appliances adorned the kitchen. The place wasn't much to speak of, but there were some interesting full-size canvases on the wall.

"Is that your artwork?" I asked.

Nolan nodded. "What do you think?"

"I like them," I said, even though I really didn't.

"You're not going to bust me for a little weed, are you?" he asked when he saw me look at the bong and the baggie of herb on the coffee table.

"That's not what I'm interested in."

Nolan seemed to breathe a little easier.

We gave a quick look around the apartment. There weren't any printing presses, and only a low-quality inkjet printer. Something that wouldn't have been capable of printing a high-quality counterfeit.

"I'd like to take a look at all the cash you have on hand," Foster said.

"It's not much," Nolan replied. "I don't think I have any more hundreds, but I'll look."

We followed him into the bedroom, and he pointed to a drawer in the dresser. "I've got some cash in there."

Foster searched the drawer. There were a few hundred dollars in 20s, 10s, and 5s.

Foster examined each of the bills, holding them up to the light, looking for the watermark. She pulled a small UV flashlight from her pocket and examined the bills.

They all seemed authentic.

"You think the guy that bought my guitar is making the bills?"

I shrugged.

"I mean, that money could have been in circulation for a while. The average person wouldn't pick up on it. I certainly didn't. It was obviously high quality."

"No telling how long that money could have been on the street," I said.

Nolan seemed more relaxed now, but I didn't buy his story. He knew more than he was saying. His nerves gave it away. Or maybe it was just two cops and a Fed in his apartment with a 1/4 ounce of weed on the coffee table.

I gave him a card, thanked him for his cooperation, then left. We walked back toward the stairs and descended into the courtyard.

Nolan peered through the blinds, watching us go.

"He's involved in something shady," JD muttered.

"I think he's a moron," Foster said. "Creative, but he doesn't have what it takes to pull something like this off. I don't buy the guitar story, but... who knows?" she said with a sigh. "I'm going to see if I can get a warrant to tap his phone, but I'm not holding my breath."

"Keep us posted," I said as she walked to her car and hopped in.

Foster was unimpressed.

We watched her drive off, and I dialed Isabella as we climbed into the Porsche. "I need another favor."

"What is it this time?"

I asked her to look into Nolan's background and cell history. "Keep tabs on him. See who he's talking to. Listen to his phone calls."

Her fingers tapped the keys, and she pulled up his information. "Counterfeiting seems way out of his league. He's got priors for shoplifting, possession, and a DUI." She paused for a moment as she dug deeper. "Looks like he failed out of art school."

"How do you fail out of art school?"

"I think you've got to try really hard. Something tells me this guy doesn't have a lot of follow-through. According to his employment record, he doesn't seem to stick with any one job for very long."

"Where is he working now?"

"Looks like he's a stocker at the grocery store."

"He's not paying rent on this island stocking groceries, I can tell you that."

"Maybe he's got a side hustle or two."

"Maybe that side hustle involves counterfeit hundred-dollar bills," I said.

Her fingers tapped the keyboard again. "Judging by the call history, it looks like you two have a mutual friend."

"I know. Sasha."

"It seems they talk quite a bit. There have been a lot of calls and texts between them recently."

"They went to art school together."

"Are you sure that's all it is?"

My face tightened with concern. "I'm not sure of anything."

"What's your involvement with Sasha?"

"Casual acquaintance," I said in an innocent voice.

"How casual?" she asked, knowing what my reply would be.

"We may have..."

Isabella sighed. "What am I going to do with you?"

"Hey, one thing led to another. And we don't know if her art school friend is mixed up with counterfeiters."

"You're right. We don't know anything yet. Maybe somebody just passed the bills to him during an exchange."

I had to admit, "He seemed way too squirrelly."

"Oh, hey. It looks like Nolan's calling Sasha right now. I'm gonna drop in on the call. I'll call you back."

37

"Want the good news or the bad news?" Isabella asked when she called back.

"Let's hear the good news," I said.

"I lied. There is no good news."

I stifled a groan. "How bad is it?"

"Well, think of it this way. At least you're getting some answers. You may not like the answers, but it is what it is. I'm gonna send you a recording of their call. You won't be able to use any of this, but at least you'll know where to focus your efforts. I also did some digging into Nolan's call history. He's made several phone calls to a prepaid cellular on the island. I was able to pinpoint the location of that prepaid device, and it happens to coincide with the location of Viktor Nevsky's superyacht. He's a—"

"I know."

"Sorry. I hate to be the bearer of bad news."

I thanked her for the information and ended the call. My phone buzzed with an MP3 a moment later and I hesitated before pressing play. I really didn't want to hear it.

I turned up the volume, and JD and I listened to it as we cruised across the island, the top down, the wind swirling.

"Hey, we might have a problem?" Nolan said.

"What kind of problem?" Sasha replied.

"Your cop friend just showed up at my apartment."

"Tyson?"

"Yeah. Whatever his name is. And that friend of his." Nolan left out the part about the Secret Service Agent.

"Why would they come to your apartment?"

Nolan hesitated for a long moment. I don't think he wanted to admit to Sasha that he had used counterfeit bills to buy drugs.

"I... I made a mistake," he stammered.

"What did you do?" Sasha asked in a severe tone—a tone that could strike fear into most people.

"I got confused, and I must have spent one of the bills."

"You did what!?" Sasha asked, flying off the handle.

"It was an honest mistake."

"Those were sample bills that were supposed to be given to Viktor."

"I know. I gave him one. He wants to do the deal. I told him there are way more where this came from. But there's a catch."

"What catch?"

"He noticed a flaw right away."

"What flaw?"

"Something about the serial numbers."

Sasha was silent for a long moment. "Where did you spend the samples?"

"What does it matter?"

"It matters."

"I don't know. I don't really remember."

"Don't lie to me!"

"I swear. I don't remember."

"Okay, I'm going to call bullshit on so many levels." She paused. Then it dawned on her. "You used it to buy drugs, didn't you?"

Nolan was silent for a moment, and his silence was all she needed.

"I don't fucking believe you," Sasha said, irate. "You're such a fuckup."

"Look, I'm the one with a connection to Viktor. You wouldn't even have this deal if it wasn't for me." He paused. "You came to me, remember? All this money and nowhere to unload it. Now we're both going to be rich."

"We're both going to be in jail because of you."

"No, we're not. They don't have shit. They searched the place and didn't find anything. I told them a story, and they bought it."

"The Secret Service is going to be all over this."

"Maybe if you'd have done a better job, we wouldn't be in this situation."

"Oh, don't turn this around on me," Sasha snapped.

"We just need to unload this stuff to Viktor and wash our hands of it."

"Did Viktor say what was wrong with the serials?"

"Something about incorrect prefixes. He offered to buy them at a discount. He can still move them."

"How much of a discount?"

There was a long moment of silence between them.

"We can talk about that. But he wants to buy a million."

"A million? That's it?"

"Look, this is a process, okay? He doesn't know you. He's never done business with you. He liked the samples, and now he wants to see if you can deliver. If all goes well, he'll scale up once you fix the issue."

"Does he know the cops are asking about the bills?"

"Hell, no! Look, we finally met last night. He loved the quality, apart from the error. Said it was the best work he'd seen in a long time. Do you know how long it took me to get that meeting?"

"Yes, I'm aware."

"I had to go through a lot of connections to get to him. He's not some guy you can just walk up to on the street. I think I deserve a little credit for that. A *thank you* would be nice."

Sasha huffed. "You're insufferable."

"You wouldn't be anywhere without me."

"When does Viktor want to do the deal?"

"I'm working on that. In the meantime, get your story straight in case your boyfriend starts asking around."

"I'm not comfortable putting flawed bills out."

"Who cares? Viktor seems to be interested. They're good enough."

"Not if the cops came around asking questions. How did they trace it back to you?"

"I don't know."

The conversation went silent for a moment.

"Are we doing the deal or not?" Nolan asked.

"I'm not sure."

"I already told him we were good to go. Don't do anything stupid. I'll call you when I hear from Viktor to set up the exchange."

That was the end of the call.

Needless to say, I was not thrilled about this new development.

"You sure can pick 'em," JD teased.

I sneered at him.

"Well, we know she's got at least a million stashed some-where, and it sounded like a hell of a lot more."

I gave a grim nod of agreement.

"How much do you think she's got?"

I shrugged.

"We can't use that audio recording," JD said. "How do you want to play this?"

"We figure out when and where that meeting with Viktor is, and we just happen to show up."

38

My phone rang with a call from Sheriff Daniels. "I just pulled Erickson and Faulkner off that surveillance detail."

My brow wrinkled with confusion. "Why?"

"Because I'm short of manpower, and it's not necessary. I got a call that someone saw Vernon at the auto show. Witness claims he was with a young woman. Matches the description of the woman he was seen with at the War Museum. Shoulder-length dark hair, early to mid-30s, pear-shaped."

"We're on it." I said. "Did you ever send anybody over to Monica's house?"

"I had Mendoza do a drive-by, but he's not sitting over there. What the hell are you two idiots doing?"

I caught him up to speed on the counterfeiting case. I may have left out a few details about my relationship with Sasha.

"Esther Pearlman is waiting for you near the entrance to the convention center," Daniels said.

I ended the call, updated JD, and we blazed the trail to the auto show.

The place was packed, and there was nowhere to park except the $40 lots nearby. Jack pulled right up to the main entrance, killed the engine, put the hazards on, and hopped out of the vehicle. The Ruby Star Porsche drew plenty of stares and looked like it should have been featured in the car show. We flashed our badges to the security guard at the entrance and told him to keep an eye on the car and not to let anybody tow it.

We stepped inside, and Esther Pearlman approached. She was in her late 50s with short, wavy dark hair that had been dyed. Her brown eyes lit up as she surveyed us. She had weathered skin and wore a white, flowing floral print dress with blue flowers. "Are you Deputies Wild and Donovan?"

I nodded and flashed my badge for good measure.

"The sheriff said you'd be coming. I was so excited when he told me he was sending you out. I've seen you both on TV."

"How long ago did you see Vernon?" I asked.

"Oh, I guess it was about half an hour ago now. He was looking at Corvettes. He was with this young woman, and at first, I thought that might have been his daughter, then it dawned on me, that's the guy everyone's looking for!"

"Was he with this woman?" I asked, showing her the sketch on my phone.

"Yes, that's her."

"Are they still here?"

She frowned and shook her head. "I got on the phone right away. The sheriff gave me his direct number when I met him at a fundraiser not too long ago," she said, almost bragging. "I called him and told him that Vernon was here, then I followed them around for a little while, keeping an eye on them." She was almost giddy with excitement. "I felt like such a spy." She giggled. Then her smile faded. "But I don't think I'd make a good spy. I think the woman noticed I was following her. She escorted Vernon out of the convention center, and I followed them to the parking lot and watched them get into this small red SUV."

I exchanged a brief glance with JD. I knew where this was going. "Did you get a license plate number?"

I did, but by the time they drove off, and I fumbled with the notes app on my phone, I forgot." She frowned again.

"That's okay. Do you recall the exact make and model of the SUV?"

"That I do know," she said with a proud smile. "It's that new Sport-4 from Toyama. Not a bad-looking car, but I like old muscle cars myself," she said with a flirty gaze.

"Thank you," I said. "This is helpful."

She smiled. "So glad to be of assistance."

JD and I started for the door when she called after us. "Oh, can I get your number, just in case I think of any other details?" she said with a wink.

I dug into my pocket and handed her a card, then JD and I dashed out of the convention center.

"I kind of wanted to look at some of the cars," Jack said.

"There's always tomorrow."

We climbed into the Porsche and hauled ass to Monica's house. The red Sport-4 was in the driveway, and the front door to her house was slightly ajar.

JD screeched to the curb. We hopped out and bolted up the walkway. I drew my pistol, and we huddled at the front door. I knocked on the door, then pushed it open. The hinges squealed, and I shouted, "Coconut County. Is anyone home?"

I got an answer to that question right away. And it wasn't the answer I was hoping for.

39

Monica lay in a pool of blood in the foyer. Crimson glistened around her body. Flat on her back, her lifeless eyes stared at the ceiling.

It looked like she had answered the door, and someone forced their way in, then put two bullets into her chest. Two spent shell casings rested on the floor near the baseboards.

There were two sets of bloody footprints around the body that trailed off toward the door.

I stepped inside with caution, making sure not to disturb any of the footprints or evidence.

Monica was long gone, but I felt for a pulse in her neck as a matter of protocol.

JD called dispatch, and we cleared the rest of the house.

There was nobody else here, and nothing appeared to be taken.

The distant warble of sirens drew near. Soon, two patrol cars pulled to the curb in front of the house, lights flashing.

Brenda and the sheriff arrived.

Dietrich snapped photos of the remains and the spent shell casings. He took close-ups of the footprints. With any luck, we'd get a make and model on the shoes.

Forensic investigators chronicled the evidence, and Brenda examined the body.

Paris Delaney and her crew had arrived. With all the commotion, a crowd of neighbors had gathered.

"Any idea when this happened?" I asked.

"This is recent," Brenda said. "I'd say within the last hour."

"Somebody had to see something," the sheriff said. "Start talking to the neighbors."

JD and I stepped outside, and Paris closed in with the camera. I answered a few brief questions, making a call for witnesses, then began to interview the bystanders. "Did anybody see anyone come or go from the house within the last hour?"

There were blank looks and head shakes all around.

"Come on," I said. "Somebody had to see or hear something."

A woman tentatively raised her hand. She was in her mid-40s and had short, curly blonde hair. She stammered, "I thought I heard two pops about 30 to 45 minutes ago. They weren't very loud. I didn't think they were loud enough to be gunshots."

"Did you happen to look out the window?" I asked.

"By the time I got a chance to look, I saw a black truck driving away. But I can't be sure if it came from Monica's."

"Did you get a license plate?"

She shook her head.

Her name was Barbara. We exchanged information, then continued to work the crowd. Nobody else had anything to add.

JD and I started banging on the neighboring doors, but that didn't turn up much, either.

We rejoined the sheriff inside the house.

"What's your take on this?" he asked.

"At this point, I'm pretty sure Monica kidnapped Vernon. She probably had help, and Mike is my prime suspect. I think they've been taking him around to museums and old car shows to jog his memory. They're trying to find out where the war bonds are."

"War bonds?"

I told him the story.

"And you think somebody showed up here at the house and kidnapped Vernon from the kidnappers?"

"That's what springs to mind."

"I thought you already searched the house."

"We did," JD said. "Vernon wasn't here."

"Get back over to the assisted living facility. Talk to the staff again. Talk to Mike. Find out what he knows. He's gotta know something."

"We're on it," I said.

We left and drove to the Sunset Palms. We caught up with Mike just as he was getting off his shift. Concern filled his eyes as we approached him in the parking lot as he stepped out of the building. "What's going on?"

"I'm afraid I have bad news for you."

His nervous eyes flicked between the two of us. "What kind of bad news?"

I told him.

He looked dumbfounded, and the color drained from his face. He didn't move for a few moments, trying to process the whole thing. "What do you mean, somebody shot her?"

"I think it's time you stop playing games with me. We know you both kidnapped Vernon. It seems that somebody took Vernon from Monica by force. We know you were after the war bonds."

He swallowed hard, and his eyes brimmed. "I want to talk to an attorney."

Innocent people don't usually ask for an attorney.

I think he was concerned more about his own preservation than he was about the loss of his girlfriend.

"You're not under arrest," I assured. I didn't have enough to go on. All I had was speculation.

"If you know everything you say you know, why am I not under arrest?"

It was a good question. I wasn't about to admit all of our *evidence* had been obtained illegally. I said nothing.

He answered for me. "That's because you don't have shit."

"At this point, I just want to get Vernon back safely. Who else knew about your little scam?"

40

M ike kept his mouth shut. He made a beeline for his car and drove off.

Paige buzzed my phone. In a frantic voice, she said, "I got another call."

"From the kidnappers?" I asked.

"This was a different person than I talked to the first time. What's going on?"

"It's a long story, but I think someone else has Vernon now," I said.

"What!?"

I told her my theory.

"They've given me 24 hours to come up with the war bonds. I'm at the storage facility now, sifting through boxes. I haven't found anything yet. I mean, they could be here. There's so much stuff."

"Which facility are you at? We'll help out."

She told me what storage space.

JD and I headed across the island, and Paige texted directions, as well as the unit number and the access code.

Coconut Storage was four stories of climate-controlled spaces. The key code allowed access 24 hours a day.

JD and I buzzed ourselves in and took the elevator up to the fourth floor. We navigated the maze of passageways, overhead fluorescent lights buzzing. Every hallway looked the same with concrete floors and steel roll-up doors. The facility was massive, and it was easy to get disoriented in a place like this. It was like a fun house that you could never escape.

At this hour, we had the place all to ourselves. All we had to do was follow Paige's sobs as they echoed down the passageways. We found her in a 10x15 unit amid a stack of boxes, tears running down her cheeks. She sat on the floor in the middle of a complete meltdown.

"Hey, are you okay?" I asked, kneeling down beside her.

She sniffled, nodded, and blotted her eyes. "I'm sorry I'm such a wreck."

"It's understandable. You're under a lot of stress right now."

"Going through all of this stuff brings back so many memories."

"Look, he's alive and well, and we're going to get him back. I promise you." I was making promises I couldn't necessarily keep. But I was determined to see Vernon's safe return.

Paige pulled herself together, and we began sorting through the boxes. There were old papers, receipts, bills, and letters.

A clothing rack in the corner held a lot of Vernon's attire. There were pictures and an old bicycle—a lifetime's worth of stuff—artifacts of a life well lived.

JD and I rooted through boxes as fast as we could.

At a cursory glance, I didn't see any war bonds in the first few boxes I went through. I didn't think that Vernon or his shipmate had made their way back to the wreckage to recover the bonds, but I had been a little bit optimistic that we might get lucky and find them here. If there *was* a map to the wreckage, it could be buried within thousands of pages of junk in the storage facility. It would take days to properly sift through everything. Even that timeline was optimistic. The boxes were stacked almost to the ceiling.

We rummaged through the boxes one by one. An hour in, I came across a box full of old journals. Each one was dated on the spine, and Vernon had kept them all the way back to his days in the war. I pulled one out, flipped it open, and began reading.

His whole life was contained in these notebooks. Day by day, he chronicled his experiences and his thoughts about what he'd seen and done. Sometimes, there were gaps of a few days. Other times, a few months. By and large, Vernon had maintained a pretty steady habit of chronicling his life.

"I think I've got something," I said to the others.

I pulled out a few notebooks and passed them around. I figured we'd start at the beginning of the war and move our way forward. If this whole story was true, I figured Vernon would have made a note of it in his journals at the time. If this was all a figment of his recent imagination, I don't think we'd find any record of it.

Once I began reading, I wanted to read more. Vernon had an engaging writing style and would have made a good author. I figured these journals could be condensed into a memoir. I wanted to take my time and sink into the stories, but time was a luxury we didn't have. I skimmed through the pages as fast as I could, looking for anything that resembled a covert mission.

It didn't take too long to get to the truth.

41

I came across a notebook that started out with the
following passage:

*I lost a few journals in the shipwreck, so I'm going to try to
re-create those entries here as best I can.*

He continued for several pages, giving a summary of the
recent events of the last few months. Then he got to the
good stuff. He talked about the covert mission and the war
bonds. He detailed how they had set out from Norfolk and
sailed along the coastline down to the Caribbean. It was in
the wee hours of the morning when two torpedoes rocked
the ship. Vernon was on watch when it happened. He said it
felt like an earthquake, the deck shifting below his feet. The
bulkheads creaked and groaned and the ship listed as it
took on water. As he recalled, the whole thing was under-
water within less than 15 minutes.

Since most of the crew were below deck, many of them
didn't get out in time. And the ones that did were left to fend
for themselves in the open ocean, clinging to anything that

would float. If that wasn't bad enough, the U-boat surfaced and began shooting at the survivors with the 88mm deck gun that was mounted on the foredeck. This made short work of the remaining crew. By some miracle, Vernon and Kenneth survived and drifted for another three days in the open ocean until they were picked up by another merchant vessel.

They were both sunburned, dehydrated, and on death's door. It was a miracle they survived at all.

Vernon drew out a detailed map and gave his estimates of the coordinates where the ship went down. The scuttlebutt among the crew prior to the sinking was that there were millions in war bonds aboard the boat, though they were never given the full details of the mission. Though Vernon wrote that he saw the war bonds locked in a safe in the captain's quarters.

I showed JD and Paige, and we studied the map.

"You think there's any truth to this?" Paige asked.

I shrugged. "I see no reason for Vernon to lie at this point."

"I don't think he intended for anyone else to read his journals," Paige said.

I called Isabella and gave her the coordinates of the supposed shipwreck. "Can you find any record of a ship going down in this area?" I told her it had left from Norfolk and gave her the approximate dates.

"Let me see what I can find."

"Were you able to track the incoming call from the second kidnappers?" I asked.

"This guy was a little smarter," Isabella said. "He used a VPN to make an Internet phone call. I was able to track it back to the Netherlands, but the VPN provider doesn't keep logs, and their security is pretty good. It would take me a while to hack their network. It's probably not worth it if they're not keeping logs."

I thanked her for the info.

After I ended the call, JD said, "I hate to be the bearer of bad news. But even if the story is true, and that map is accurate, we don't know if Kenneth ever went back for the bonds. Even if he didn't, 24 hours is not enough time to find that ship and recover whatever may be down there."

He had a point.

It seemed like an impossible situation.

42

"I've got an idea," JD said.

We both looked at him with curious eyes.

"The kidnappers want 10,000 series E war bonds," Jack said. "The series E was discontinued in 1980. I dare say that most of them have already been redeemed by now. Have you ever seen one? Held one in your hand?"

Paige and I both shook our heads.

A mischievous grin curled Jack's lips. "I'm guessing that our kidnapper has never seen one in person, either. Sure, you can find pictures on the Internet. But if any of those are still out in the wild, they're probably locked away in someone's safe or a collector's vault."

I knew where he was going with this, and it wasn't a bad idea.

"I say we take a page from your girlfriend's book and make some counterfeits."

Paige looked at me with curious eyes. "You have a girlfriend?"

"No. She was more of an acquaintance, really."

"A one-night stand," she said with a sassy eyebrow.

"Let's just say she withheld certain pertinent information about herself."

"Liars are the worst," she replied. "Sorry. I'm getting too personal."

Paige was cute, and I think she might have been a little bit interested.

"You two can flirt later," JD said. "Let's get back on track."

Paige's cheeks reddened.

"You want to counterfeit war bonds," I said to Jack. "Then exchange them for Vernon."

"Sounds like a great idea to me."

I looked at Paige. She nodded in agreement.

"How are we going to forge war bonds?"

"We could always ask Sasha for tips," Jack joked.

"Something tells me she's not going to admit to anything right now," I said.

We left the storage unit, and Paige locked up. She followed us back to the *Avventura*, and we planned out our little counterfeiting operation. Jack got online and started researching, pulling up images of series E bonds that were issued during 1941.

"Can we get in trouble for doing this?" Paige asked.

"Technically, we're forging registered securities. A government document," I said. "There are pretty hefty penalties for this kind of thing."

The whole thing sparked an idea. It might not have been a good idea, but it was an idea, nonetheless.

I called Agent Foster. "I have some information you might be interested in."

"I'm all ears."

"I've acquired some evidence. Inadmissible evidence."

"Okay," she said, drawing it out in an uncertain voice. "Do I want to know how you acquired this inadmissible evidence?"

"No. But I think I might be able to deliver Viktor Nevsky to you."

"Do that, and you'll become my new favorite person."

"But I need a favor."

"Nothing in life is free, is it?"

I told her about the phone call between Nolan and Sasha, then updated her on the situation with Vernon.

"So, let me get this straight. You want me to come up with 10,000 series E war bonds, each with a face value of $10,000? And you want me to do that by tomorrow?"

"So, we're on the same page," I said with an optimistic grin.

"That's a tall order. I don't know if it's possible. Those bonds haven't been printed since 1980."

"I know. I just need a reasonable facsimile. Something that would pass initial observation."

She laughed. "Are you seriously asking a Secret Service Agent to counterfeit Treasury Bonds?"

"Yes, I believe so."

She laughed again. "You're bold, if nothing else. I'll give you that."

"Fortune favors the bold," I said, quoting the Latin proverb.

"What do you think? Is it doable?"

Foster sighed. "Let me make some phone calls and see what I can do. In the meantime, I want you to keep me posted on this Nevsky thing. I assume you're staying on top of that."

"I've got my hands full at the moment, but if you want to put surveillance on Sasha and Nolan, be my guest. Just don't get spotted, or you'll blow the deal."

"Believe me, I'm not about to screw this up. I'm ready for a little payback."

43

"**D**o you think she's gonna come through?" Paige asked with concerned eyes.

"I hope so," I replied.

"I don't think we should sit on our hands, waiting for her to save the day," JD added. "We need to get on this ASAP."

I agreed.

"You're the graphic expert," he said. "Why don't you work on coming up with the design while I go to the office supply store and get some quality paper and other materials?"

JD took off, and I went to work on my laptop. I really wanted to call Sasha and ask her for some pointers, but I didn't want to tip my hand.

The design of the war bond was a lot less complex than modern currency. I was able to find a high-resolution image online. After researching the exact dimensions and enhancing the image in a graphics program, I had a reasonable reproduction. The only problem was all the serial numbers would be the same. I used the photo editing program to manipulate the numbers and came up with about two dozen unique serial numbers. From these master files, we could print batches and shuffle them so that, upon a cursory glance, they would all look like individual bonds. This wouldn't fool a bank, and certainly not a treasury agent, but it might fool a kidnapper long enough to make the exchange.

JD returned with boatloads of resume paper that was thicker and embedded with fibers. It sort of resembled bond paper, but anyone who knew anything about series E bonds wouldn't buy it. All we had to do was pass initial muster— just long enough to do the swap.

Or so I hoped.

I showed him the images that I had prepared, and he gave me a thumbs-up. Paige seemed satisfied, and we began our little counterfeiting operation, printing off the bonds two to a sheet. Once I printed the initial test sheet, we flipped it over and printed the back of the bond. It took a couple tries to get the registration to line up perfectly so the front and the back matched. After a few tries, we got pretty close. Close enough for government work.

JD had gotten buckets of ink for the printer and a paper cutter. We went to work printing, and our makeshift press ran all night.

But it wasn't without its issues. We had some print clogs and some banding issues with the printer. After a few head cleanings, things got back on track.

We printed, trimmed, and stacked the bonds neatly. It was a

massive undertaking and took all night. It was sunrise when the inkjet spit out the last bond.

We just had one slight problem.

The ink in this printer wasn't waterproof. And these were bonds that had supposedly been submerged in water for the last 80 years. We needed to distress and age the bonds somehow. Our counterfeits looked brand new.

This certainly wouldn't do.

We tried to soak one of them in water, but the ink bled enough to make it look like an obvious fake.

All that work for nothing.

In our excitement, we had forgotten to test for that one simple thing. Even if the ink had been waterproof, there probably wasn't enough time to dry the bonds anyway.

"What the hell are we gonna do?" Paige asked.

"Fake it till we make it," JD said.

"They're going to know these aren't real."

"I'm guessing this is the first time they've done something like this," Jack said. "They're going to be so nervous that they're gonna take the money and run."

"I hope you're right," Paige said with a worried sigh.

"I'll call Agent Foster," I said. "Hopefully, she's made some progress."

I dialed her number, but she didn't answer. It went to voice-mail. "Hey, just touching base. We're coming up on the deadline, and we sure could use your assistance. Call me back at your earliest convenience."

44

The day came and went, and I didn't hear a peep from Agent Foster. I had pretty much given up hope on that avenue.

It was the late afternoon when Paige got a call from the kidnappers. She put it on speakerphone, and we huddled around, listening to the instructions.

"Do you have the bonds?" the voice asked, cackling through the phone.

"I do," Paige replied.

"I want you to take them out to Crystal Key. Put them in a duffel bag, and leave them on the diving board at the resort pool."

The resort at Crystal Key had long since been abandoned. Several hurricanes had demolished the island, and the resort that had been under construction was left in disarray. It had been vacant for years and was now home to vagrants, the occasional drug deal, and kids looking for a place to party. It was probably as good a place as any to make an exchange.

"I want to speak with my grandfather," Paige demanded.

"Bring the bonds, and you'll get to speak with him."

"No!" Paige said in a forceful tone. "You put him on the phone now, or you'll never see the war bonds."

I couldn't help but smirk. I liked her spunk. She had guts, and she was not going to let this asshole back her down.

The phone rustled for a moment, then Vernon said, "Hello?"

"Grandpa?" Paige asked, her voice quivering.

"Hey, sweetie!"

"Are you okay?"

"I'm fine."

"This is all going to be over with soon," she assured.

The kidnapper yanked the phone away from Vernon as he muttered something.

"Bring the bonds at 10 o'clock. Not a minute later. No cops. If I see anyone else, the old man dies."

Vernon muttered something in the background.

"I don't have a boat," Paige said. "I'm gonna have a friend bring me out there."

The kidnapper grumbled. "Fine. But that's it. Nobody else."

That was the end of the call.

"Do you recognize his voice?" I asked.

Paige shook her head.

A few nervous hours passed, and the sun set over the horizon.

JD and I prepped the tender with weapons, night vision optics, and just about everything we might need. I had pulled it out of the garage and tied it up at the dock. It wasn't quite as fast or powerful as our old wake boat, but it would get the job done. It was a real boat, not a rigid inflatable. We donned camouflage tactical gear and were ready for just about anything.

The time to depart drew near.

My phone buzzed with a call from Agent Foster.

"Please tell me you've got good news," I said.

45

I t was cutting it close.

JD and I waited at the end of the dock for Agent Foster to arrive. She pulled in, driving a black SUV with tinted windows, and drove around to the dock. She pulled alongside JD and me and rolled down the passenger window as she popped the back hatch. The hydraulics lifted it open.

"What you asked for is in the back," she shouted through the open window. "The serial numbers have been logged, and there are tracking chips embedded within the duffel bag. It was too short notice to put them into the bonds. But if these clowns show up anywhere and try to cash them out, we will get notified."

I breathed a sigh of relief. "Thank you."

"You owe me. You better come through with Nevsky."

"You have a surveillance team on Sasha and Nolan?"

Jack moved to the back of the vehicle, grabbed the duffel bag, and closed the hatch. He lugged the oversized duffel full of bonds back to the dock, dropped it on the ground with a thunk, and unzipped it. His eyes gleamed as he looked upon the perfect forgeries. You couldn't get better counterfeit bonds than ones made by the US Government.

"I couldn't get a warrant to tap their phones," Foster said with more than a trace of doubt in her voice. "I've got no probable cause for any of this."

"Trust me. Those two will lead to Viktor Nevsky."

She looked uncertain but hopeful.

"We gotta run," I said.

"Good luck," she shouted as JD zipped up the bag.

We lugged the bonds down the dock. He took one handle, and I took the other to lighten the load. It had to weigh close to 70 pounds.

We tossed the duffel bag aboard the tender, then hopped in. The bonds still looked brand new, but hopefully the kidnappers would be too greedy to notice.

Paige boarded the boat, and I cast off the lines. JD took the helm and cruised us out of the marina. We cleared the breakwater and JD brought the boat on plane. The boat sliced through the inky swells, the moon glowing the water. The engines howled, and the briny air whipped across the bow. We raced into the abyss, leaving the island behind.

Paige looked tense, her face tight and full of anticipation. I tried to reassure her, but these kinds of exchanges were always uncertain at best.

It didn't take long to get to Crystal Key. As we approached, I grabbed the night vision optics and moved to the bow. I scanned the island, looking for signs of life, but the place was desolate.

Jack circled the island before pulling into the shallows on the south side. We dropped anchor, and I hopped out into the surf.

"You should probably stay on the boat," I suggested to Paige.

Her face wrinkled. "No! I'm going with you. They're expecting me, not you."

She hopped out of the boat, and JD handed me the duffel bag, then followed.

We trudged through the surf to the beach and advanced to the tree line. Once again, I scanned the island with IR optics.

I didn't identify any targets.

JD and I put in wireless earbuds and connected through a secure app on our phones, giving us encrypted comms.

After a quick radio check, Jack took off to the east, running along the tree line with his sniper rifle. He darted into the underbrush and looked for a good position to set up overwatch.

Paige and I took the path up to the main resort. The asphalt trail was cracked and uneven. Weeds sprouted through the gaps, and the island was doing a pretty good job of reclaiming its turf. In a few years, there would be no trace left.

The exterior of the main lobby was covered in graffiti. The doors and windows had been boarded up, but many of those had long since been torn down. The panes of glass had been shattered, and shards littered the ground around the window frames. The swimming pool was an algae-filled mosquito paradise. There wasn't much left of the lounge chairs. The sun and elements had done their damage, and many of them ended up at the bottom of the *lagoon* that attempted to pass for a pool.

A phone rang nearby.

The display glowed with an incoming call. The device rested atop the diving board.

Paige and I hustled around the green water, and she picked up the phone. She swiped the screen and took the call. In a tentative voice, she said, "Hello?"

"Leave the bonds on the diving board," the voice said. It was a video call, but the screen was blank on the kidnapper's end.

"No," Paige said. "Not until I have Vernon."

"Once you leave the bonds, we'll release Vernon."

"It doesn't work that way," Paige said.

"It works how I say it works."

I scanned the area, looking for the perps. I thought they might be hiding somewhere within view. They seemed to know the instant we arrived poolside. Perhaps they had some type of camera set up, transmitting the feed over a cellular network to their location.

A faint buzzing sound overhead drew my attention. A small black drone hovered high in the air, capturing us on video.

The drone operator had to be within range—perhaps a mile or two.

"Open the duffel bag," the voice commanded through the phone. "I want to see the bonds."

I unzipped the duffel bag, pulled it open, and displayed the bonds. Paige turned the camera around and filmed the bonds within, flipping through them to show they were all legit and not just stacked atop blank paper.

"Leave the bonds, return to your boat, and get off the island. Take the cell phone with you and leave it on at all times. By the time you get back to Coconut Key, Vernon will be a free man."

"I'm supposed to take your word on that?" Paige said, incredulous.

"What choice do you have?"

The kidnapper disconnected the call.

Paige looked at me with worried eyes. "What do we do?"

"He's right," I said. "We don't have many options now."

I grabbed the phone the kidnappers had left. I had no doubt they were tracking the device and wanted to keep tabs on our whereabouts. The phone could also be used to listen in on our conversations. I didn't know how tech-savvy these kidnappers were, but so far, they were doing things right.

Paige started, "What if—"

I stopped her before she asked the obvious question. I just shook my head and looked up.

She saw the drone.

I kept my head on a swivel, scanning the area as we returned to the shore.

JD crackled through my earbud. "Do you want me to sit here and see who shows up?"

"That's a negative," I said.

There was no doubt they'd watched us arrive. I didn't want to do anything to jeopardize Vernon's safe return at this point. The kidnappers were probably sitting offshore, but we hadn't spotted any other vessels in the area.

JD joined us on the beach, and we waded into the surf. We climbed aboard the boat, weighed anchor, and Jack took the helm, navigating us back toward Coconut Key. It was loud enough to obscure our conversation if they were listening through the phone.

Paige hissed in my ear, "What if they discover the bonds are fake?"

I shook my head. "Those are as authentic as any forgeries are going to get."

"What if they just dump Vernon on the street? How will I ever find him?"

She was in panic mode now, and that was understandable. I'm sure the ride back to Coconut Key was agonizing for her.

46

We pulled into the marina at Diver Down, and JD navigated us into a slip. I tied off, then helped Paige ashore. As we walked down the dock toward the *Avventura*, her phone buzzed with a call.

Her reflexes were lightning. She answered before the first ring ended. "Hello?"

"You'll find Vernon at the old lighthouse," the voice said.

"You just left him in the street!?" Paige snapped.

"Be thankful we let him go."

The call disconnected, and we rushed down the dock to the Porsche. JD hopped behind the wheel, and Paige climbed into the backseat. It was pretty tiny back there, and I would never have fit.

He cranked up the engine, pulled out of the space, then tore out of the parking lot. Jack raced across the island to the lighthouse.

Vernon ambled down the sidewalk a block away, looking disoriented.

JD pulled to the curb alongside him, and I hopped out.

Paige followed, running to Vernon and giving him a hug. "Grandpa!"

He looked startled and confused but returned the hug.

"Oh, thank God you're okay," she said with a relieved breath.

He squinted at her. "Paige?"

She smiled through tears of joy. "Yes, it's me."

"Why wouldn't I be okay?"

"You were kidnapped?"

His face wrinkled. "I was?"

She nodded.

He considered it for a moment.

"You remember anything about the last few days?"

"I recall I had a lot of fun. More fun than I've had in a long time. We went to the museum, to the auto show, and we went to a strip club," he said with a mischievous grin.

Paige frowned at him.

Vernon looked at me with confusion.

"Grandpa, I'd like you to meet my friend, Tyson Wild. He's a deputy with Coconut County."

"Pleasure to meet you, young man," he said, extending his hand.

We shook. Vernon had a firm grasp.

"Do you think you could describe your companions over the last few days?" I asked.

"Sure," he said.

I waited for him to continue.

His face wrinkled as he thought about it. "Well, I'm not quite sure. It will come to me," he said, dismissing his memory lapse.

"Let's get you back to the Sunset Palms," Paige said.

His face wrinkled. "I don't want to go back to the Sunset Palms."

"But that's where you live," Paige said.

"No, it's not. I live on Mercury Street."

"You moved, remember?"

Vernon thought about it for a moment. "I reckon I did."

"I don't think the Sunset Palms is the best place for him at the moment," I said.

"Right," Paige said. She addressed Vernon in a soothing voice. "Come on. We're going to take you home." She gave him a hug. "I love you, Grandpa."

He hugged her back. "I love you, too."

I think that was all she needed to hear. Her eyes misted with tears of joy.

I called for a rideshare. There wasn't enough room for the four of us in the Porsche. Getting Vernon in and out of the low-slung sports car would have been a task. I requested an SUV, and the driver picked us up a few minutes later.

We took Vernon back to Paige's apartment.

I helped Paige get Vernon into her unit.

"You think you can manage him on your own?" I asked once he was situated.

Paige nodded. "I can get through the night, then figure out a more permanent solution."

"I'm just a phone call away if you need anything."

She smiled. "I really appreciate that," she said, then gave me a hug.

She was a good hugger.

I said goodbye to Vernon, and we shook hands again. "It was a pleasure to meet you, sir. You've got a wonderful grand-daughter who loves you very much."

"What can I say? I'm a lucky man."

Before I left, I asked Vernon about the war bonds, and he went into specifics about his covert mission. He either remembered everything in striking detail, or he was a hell of a storyteller. I'm not sure which. But listening to him, I got the distinct impression that the story was true. I think Vernon could have gone on for hours, telling stories. He was a fascinating man who lived a full life.

"Okay, that's enough stories for one evening," Paige said.

"Come back anytime," Vernon said. "There's more where that came from."

I asked him one more time about the kidnappers.

"Well, they all wore disguises. But they weren't fooling anybody."

"So you recognized them?"

"Hell, yes," Vernon said. "Monica and Mike took me out of the facility in the middle of the night. We hung out for a few days on Monica's sailboat. That was fun. Then I guess she did something to make Otis mad 'cause he shot her," he said with a frown. "He took me from her place, but I wasn't going to argue. He had a gun."

I pulled out my phone and recorded his statement. "Can you repeat that?"

He did and didn't miss a beat.

"Otis always wore a mask, but I knew it was him," Vernon said. "Recognized the voice."

"Thank you. This is helpful."

I said my goodbyes, and Paige escorted me out of the apartment. She pulled the door shut behind her, and we talked in the hall for a moment. "Will you be able to use his testimony?"

"I'm going down to the station now. I'll fill out an application for a warrant and hopefully make some arrests."

"What if Vernon doesn't remember anything in a few days?"

"That could be a problem," I admitted.

This was an opportunity to put the perpetrators behind bars, at least for a short time. It would put the pressure on Mike.

Paige gave me another hug, and I didn't mind.

I hustled down the hallway and called the sheriff. I caught a rideshare down to the station where I filled out an application for a warrant.

47

T he judge signed off on a warrant for Mike, but not for Otis. Vernon never saw his face, and apparently, that was a deal-breaker.

We gathered outside Mike's apartment with a tactical team. I banged on the door and shouted, "Coconut County! We have a warrant."

CRACK!

CRUNCH!

SNAP!

Faulkner heaved the battering ram against the door, and it flung wide, scattering splinters.

I led the way into the foyer, and the team followed. I cleared the kitchen and advanced into the living room. My barrel swept across the area, then I advanced toward the bedroom door. It was closed.

JD and I huddled on either side, and I shouted again, "Coconut County!"

Commotion inside filtered through the door.

I took a step back and kicked it open.

The door rattled and swung wide, the doorknob digging into the drywall.

JD and I pushed into the bedroom with caution, clearing the corners.

Mike was halfway out the window.

From the second story, it wasn't that much of a drop, but Mike had second thoughts about it. His wide eyes stared at the ground, then flicked to us.

"Freeze!" I shouted.

He didn't listen.

Mike climbed out of the window. He hung down and let go.

The action was followed by a thump, a crack, and a groan of agony.

I rushed to the window and angled my pistol at the perp below.

Mike lay on the ground moaning, clutching his leg, which was bent at an unnatural angle.

I shouted back through the apartment at Erickson and Faulkner. "He's on the ground!"

They raced out of the apartment, and it didn't take them long to circle around behind the building and secure the suspect.

I called dispatch and had them send EMTs and paramedics.

Soon, the area swarmed with first responders.

Mike's cute neighbor stepped outside and watched the chaos with curiosity.

EMTs treated Mike, then loaded him onto a gurney and rolled him around to the parking lot. By that time, Paris Delaney was on the scene. She got a nice shot of them stuffing Mike into the back of an ambulance.

She asked me for a comment, but I declined.

The morning sun had crested the horizon, and I was ready for bed. JD and I filled out after-action reports at the station, then we hit Waffle Wizard on the way back to the *Avventura*. I figured I'd catch a power nap, then interview Mike in the afternoon. But fate had other plans.

I took Buddy out for a quick walk before I settled in. I was out the minute my head hit the pillow, but I had no sooner gotten to sleep when the phone rang. I grabbed the evil thing from the nightstand and looked at the screen.

I needed to take this call.

"What's going on?" I asked.

"Nolan just called Sasha," Isabella said. "Viktor wants to do the deal tonight. But there's a slight problem."

"What?"

"Sasha doesn't want to do the deal with Viktor until she can correct the error and print more. She wants to destroy the existing batch. You need to sort this thing out before she destroys the evidence."

I thanked her for the info, then ended the call. I pulled myself out of bed and dialed Special Agent Foster.

She answered after a few rings. "How did everything work out?"

"We got Vernon back."

"Glad to hear it. What about the bonds?"

"I'm sure those will turn up."

"We lost the GPS signal on the bag before you left the marina."

"You still have eyes on Sasha and Nolan?"

"I've got two agents sitting in a van outside her apartment and an agent sitting in the parking lot across the street from Nolan's building. Not much is happening. They're about to throw in the towel."

"Well, things might be about to heat up," I said, then told her what Isabella had told me.

"How reliable is your intel?"

"As good as it gets."

"How are you getting this information? Have you tapped their phones?"

"I can neither confirm nor deny."

"And who's doing this for you?"

"You shouldn't ask questions that you don't want answers to."

"You realize you could jeopardize this entire operation by acquiring evidence illegally."

"I haven't done anything illegal. The intel just happened to fall in my lap."

She sighed. "What's the next move?"

"If we get lucky, I think Sasha's going to lead us to the money."

48

J D and I swapped the Porsche for the surveillance van at the station. Agent Foster joined us, and we headed over to Sasha's apartment.

Foster had cut her people loose. They'd been there for the last eight hours and were ready for a break.

The surveillance van was wrapped with the logo of a fake plumbing company. Inside was every imaginable surveillance gadget. There were large flatscreen displays pumping in video feeds from the external high-definition cameras. Laser microphones could hear conversations inside a house, picking up vibrations on the windows. There was a mini fridge, a small portable restroom, and a surveillance drone that could be launched from the roof of the vehicle. It was state-of-the-art, and since JD had funded the little adventure, no expense was spared. Still, it didn't take long for the tiny van to make you go stir-crazy.

"This is nicer than ours," Foster said.

JD grinned. "Maybe someday you can have all the resources the county has."

She gave him a flat look.

JD sat at the computer terminal and angled a camera at the entrance to Sasha's apartment complex. Another was aimed at the gate to the under-building parking.

Isabella had been tracking Sasha's phone, and it was still at her apartment.

It was a little after noon when Sasha pulled out of the parking garage in her Cybertruck.

"Looks like we're Oscar Mike," JD said.

I hopped behind the wheel, cranked up the engine, then followed the space-age truck. I kept my distance and put a few cars in between us, but it wouldn't take long for her to notice a bright green plumbing van following her.

Sasha meandered through the city and ended up in the warehouse district, not too far from the practice studio. She pulled into a parking lot surrounded by a chain-link fence topped with razor wire. She parked the truck by the loading dock, hopped out, and climbed the steps. Keys jingled as she fumbled to unlock the door, then stepped inside.

I parked the van a little way down the street, but with a clear view of the parking lot of the warehouse.

"That's where she's keeping the money," Foster said. "If what you say is true, she's going to destroy all of it, and there's not a damn thing we can do about it."

We sat in the van, watching, hoping for probable cause. Mixed feelings bounced around inside me. I liked Sasha.

She was a nice girl and a lot of fun. There was a part of me that hoped this was all some big misunderstanding. But there was no denying what was going on.

Sasha emerged from the warehouse, lugging a green lawn-size trash bag. She carried it down the dock and hefted it into the open green dumpster, then returned inside.

Foster's eyes lit up with glee as we watched on the flatscreen displays. "That's trash. Trash is fair game."

"That's trash on private property," I said.

"That waste bin is the property of the garbage company."

"It's still on private property."

A *No Trespassing* sign on the gate clearly indicated this was not a public area. Even by throwing the bag into the trash, Sasha still had a reasonable expectation of privacy. JD and I had been through a similar scenario before in a recent case.

"Anything we get out of that dumpster now would be inadmissible in court," I said.

Foster gave me a look, then snarked, "I didn't realize you guys were so by the book."

JD feigned offense. "What? Do you think we just bend the rules to suit our fancy?"

I'm not sure how he kept a straight face.

Her eyes narrowed at him. "You guys have probably broken every rule in the book."

Sasha emerged with another bag, then another.

Then she returned with lighter fluid and doused the contents of the dumpster. When she'd emptied the container of fluid, she tossed it in the bin, then pulled a pack of bar matches from her pocket.

She lit a match, and the flame flickered, then blew out with the wind.

Not to be deterred, she lit another and set the whole pack of matches on fire. The matches flared.

The evidence was about to go up in smoke.

49

WHOOSH!

The pack of matches sparked a furious inferno. Flames roared, launching out of the dumpster, swirling black smoke into the sky.

Sasha backed away, the heat growing intense. She moved inside the warehouse, returned with two more bags, and tossed them into the blazing pit of hell.

She hurried back inside for more. She must have had a ton of counterfeit money stashed in that place.

JD grinned. "You know what that is, ladies and gentlemen?"

"That's evidence going up in flames," Foster said, gnashing her teeth.

"No. That's arson. That's illegal. That's probable cause."

I called dispatch and had them alert the fire department, then we hustled out of the van and ran toward the warehouse. We rushed inside the gate as Sasha emerged with two more bags.

Her eyes rounded.

She froze in her tracks for an instant, then kept walking toward the dumpster. Then she asked in a flustered voice, "Tyson, what are you doing here?"

"Drop the bags."

"What?" she asked innocently.

By this time, Agent Foster had drawn her weapon. She wasn't playing around. "Drop the bags, now!"

The distant sounds of sirens warbled, drawing near.

I guess Sasha was a gambling type of girl because she tossed the bags into the dumpster.

Foster didn't shoot her, but I think she wanted to.

"On the ground, now!" Foster shouted.

"I don't understand this. What's going on?"

"You're under arrest for arson," I said.

"You can't be serious," Sasha said like it was absurd. "I'm on private property."

I explained to her that you couldn't just set a dumpster on fire, but I'm sure the definition of *arson* would be contested.

"I can't believe you're going to arrest me for something so silly. Who's the victim here? Who does this hurt?"

"Save it, sweetheart," Foster said. "Get on the ground now! You're about to have a lot bigger problems than arson."

Sasha looked at me with sad eyes, confused by the betrayal.

I felt like an ass.

JD climbed the dock and cuffed her. He was gentle about it. He helped her to her feet and Mirandized her as he escorted her down the steps.

The fire raged on, smoke filling the sky. Embers drifted about.

The fire department finally arrived and doused the flames. It didn't take much to put out the fire.

Paris Delaney and crew arrived just in time to catch the last of the flames.

Wisps of smoke drifted from the dumpster, and the smell of soggy ash filled the air. The steel bin popped and hissed as it cooled.

Patrol units had arrived, lights flickering.

JD escorted Sasha to a patrol car and stuffed her in the back. She ignored me and kept a vigilant watch on Agent Foster as she approached the smoldering dumpster. Foster peered in through a side hatch and looked at the remains.

Despite the intense flames, partially burned bills remained. It would be more than enough to put Sasha away for 20 years.

She was taken to the station, processed, printed, and put into an interrogation room.

We searched the warehouse and found printing presses, ink, and paper.

We headed back to the station. JD and I filled out after-action reports in the conference room.

Agent Foster wanted to interview her.

"I know her," I said. "She might be more willing to talk to me."

Foster lifted a curious eyebrow. I had left that detail out. "You know her?"

"It's a small island."

"How well do you know her?"

A guilty expression tugged my face. "Pretty well."

Foster sighed, picking up on just how well I knew Sasha. "You can't go near this case. You're personally involved with the suspect. A defense attorney would have a field day with that."

I raised my hands innocently. "Alright, it's all you."

She glared at me, not pleased.

JD and I watched from the observation room as Agent Foster stepped into the interrogation room and took a seat across the table from Sasha. The overhead fluorescent lights buzzed, and the two stared each other down in the tiny room.

Foster introduced herself and displayed her credentials. "You're being charged with second-degree arson and possession of counterfeit money. You're looking at 20 years behind bars."

Foster let that hang there for a moment.

Sasha swallowed hard but remained stone-faced and stared the agent down. "I want to speak with an attorney."

Sasha was no dummy.

That was the end of the interview.

Foster made an ominous face, pushed away from the table, and stepped into the hallway.

JD and I joined her with the sheriff a moment later.

"You have a limited amount of time before Nolan figures out she's been arrested," I said. "You can kiss Viktor Nevsky goodbye if you don't get information from her."

Foster's face tensed.

"If the arson case gets tossed, this whole case goes up in flames," Daniels reminded. "Odds are good, it goes bye-bye. A defense attorney is going to argue that based on your prior relationship, this was a vendetta. A jilted lover scorned."

"I wasn't jilted."

The sheriff sneered at me.

"How was I supposed to know she was counterfeiting money?" I said, in my defense.

The sheriff's annoyed gaze persisted.

I raised my hands innocently. "This isn't even my area. I'm more than happy to leave the counterfeiting to the experts."

That drew an irritated look from Agent Foster.

"I'm no attorney, but this case is going to come down to whether she created a risk to person or property," I said.

"That dumpster is the property of the waste management company," Foster replied. "There is an argument that it was damaged by the flames and needs to be reconditioned. Perhaps the structural integrity is compromised, thus leading to safety issues in the removal of waste product. That, on its face, fulfills the definition of 2nd Degree Arson."

"The clock is ticking," I said. "That's all I'm saying. The longer she sits in there, the more people on the outside are going to start to wonder."

After another long, tense moment, Agent Foster said. "Go in there and talk to her. See what you can get out of her. You've already screwed the pooch on this case. I don't see how you could make it any worse."

I gave her a look. "What concessions are you willing to offer?"

"I'm not in a position to offer anything," she said. "That's up to the Assistant US Attorney."

"I'm sure your recommendation would have considerable influence."

Foster thought about it for a moment, then told me her terms.

I pushed into the interrogation room, and Sasha glared at me as I walked to the table and took a seat across from her.

"You're such an asshole." The words rolled off her slick tongue with venom. "How could you do this to me?"

"I think you did it to yourself when you printed those counterfeit bills."

The muscles in her jaw flexed. "I asked for a lawyer. You have to stop questioning me. I know my rights."

"I'm not questioning you. I'm merely here to let you know that you're looking at considerable jail time. But there might be a way out."

That piqued her curiosity. After a moment, she said, "I'm listening."

"The Feds are interested in Viktor Nevsky. He's a bigger fish than you are."

She stared me down and processed the information. "Go on."

"You're in a unique position right now. He doesn't know you've been arrested, and he still believes you have something he wants."

She knew where I was going with this. "You want me to go through with my meeting so you can arrest him."

"I knew you were a smart girl. The question is, will you be smart enough to take the deal?"

"What's the deal?"

50

"The arson charges get dropped," I said. "You confess to the counterfeiting, help us bag Viktor Nevsky and anyone else involved in your production process, and you serve 15 years in a minimum-security prison."

She scoffed. "15 years?"

"Beats 20."

"Not by much."

For someone in her position, I was surprised to see a slight smirk on her plump lips. "My dad always told me never to take the first deal somebody offered. And that deal is complete dog shit."

"I'm trying to help you."

Her face wrinkled. "If you cared at all about me, you wouldn't have arrested me."

"Technically, I didn't arrest you. And nobody forced you to make counterfeit bills."

She frowned. "I'm not admitting to anything. Hypothetically speaking... *If* I did as you claim, and I were to help you, I would expect to walk away with no jail time and no fine. My record stays clean. I give you Viktor Nevsky and the details of my alleged process."

I could almost hear Agent Foster laughing in the observation room.

"I'll pass that along, but I don't think that will be acceptable."

"I've got a little cookie to sweeten the deal," she said.

"What's that?"

"What would you say if I could tell you where there's another hundred million dollars in counterfeit bills? Certainly, the Secret Service doesn't want that in circulation." She leaned back with a confident grin on her face.

I lifted a curious eyebrow. "You have another hundred million in counterfeit bills?"

"No. I said, *what if*?"

She was smart, alright.

"The bills are imperfect," I said. "You made a mistake."

"Even if I *allegedly* made a mistake, the quality of those bills is unrivaled. They would easily fool the average person. They could be used domestically or overseas. I doubt anyone in another part of the world would even notice the difference." Then, she added, "If such bills did, in fact, exist."

"Then why burn them?"

"Some people take pride in their work."

I considered it for a moment. "Let me see what I can do."

I pushed away from the table, walked to the door, and gave a quick knock. A guard buzzed me out, and I waited for the sheriff, JD, and Agent Foster to join me.

"She's full of shit," Foster said.

I shrugged. "Take her word for it, or don't. Makes no difference to me at this point. If she's lying, she doesn't get the deal."

"She's not getting that deal, anyway. No way she walks on this."

"Then Viktor Nevsky's gonna walk away."

The muscles in Foster's jaw tightened. Her eyes narrowed at me. "Whose side are you on?"

"I'm trying to help you get the man who killed your partner. That's whose side I'm on."

Foster's face reddened. She wasn't about to let Nevsky slip away. She just had to wrestle with the idea for a moment. She took a deep breath and tried to center herself. "She does 10 years, helps us get Nevsky, and hands over the hundred million that's still out there."

I shrugged. "I'll see what she says. I don't think that's going to cut it."

I stepped back into the interrogation room and laid it out for Sasha.

"Not only no, but hell no." She leaned into her power in the situation. "I can give you one of the most notorious criminals and money launderers. A guy who is not only debasing US currency but is funding terrorist operations and other criminal organizations. I'm just an artist. I'm just somebody who's trying to make the world a more beautiful place," she said with a smile. "Tell me, who's worth more to you and your people behind the glass?"

51

"I'll talk to the federal prosecutor and see what we can work out," Foster said after I joined her in the hallway.

"The clock is ticking," I reminded her.

Foster excused herself and made a phone call.

Denise found us. "DNA came back on the hair fiber found in the stolen car suspected in the Lamonte Kent shooting. No match in the database."

"What about the shell casing? Any prints?"

"No. Whoever loaded that weapon was smart enough to wear gloves."

"Rafferty lawyered up," the sheriff said. "He's not going to give anything voluntarily, and Echols denied a warrant to compel his DNA."

My face wrinkled. "Is he tight with Echols?"

"I doubt it. But he didn't find Lamonte to be the most credible witness."

"Well, we'll just have to get his DNA another way," JD said.

The sheriff surveyed us with stern eyes. "This isn't your case anymore. Let IA handle it."

"IA's not doing diddly squat," Denise said.

The muscles in the sheriff's face tightened. "Look, I don't want dirty cops on my payroll any more than anyone else does. So whatever you two do, keep it by the book. I mean it."

I gave him a mock salute, and he was not impressed.

Foster ended her call and rejoined us. "If she can give us Nevsky and a hundred million in counterfeit bills, she can walk."

"I bet that was painful to say."

She glared at me.

I excused myself and grabbed Sasha's cell phone from the property department. Then JD, Foster, and I entered the interrogation room.

"Looks like you got yourself a deal," I said.

Sasha grinned. "I don't see a piece of paper."

"They're sending the deal over," Foster said.

"I'll wait," Sasha replied with confidence.

And wait, she did.

It took 45 minutes for the paperwork to come through. Foster printed the PDF that was signed by the Assistant US Attorney and presented it to Sasha. She looked over the details. "I really should have my attorney read this first."

"We're running out of time," Foster said.

Sasha hesitated a moment, then looked at me for guidance. Not that she really trusted me anymore, but I gave a nod of approval.

"If I get screwed over..."

"This is going to be the best thing that ever happened to you," Foster said. "You're getting your life back. Not many people get a second chance."

I could relate to second chances. Having had a near-death experience, I was determined to make the most of my life. I hoped that Sasha would do the same. She had a promising career ahead of her if she focused her attention in the right direction.

Sasha signed the paperwork and then asked, "What do you need me to do?"

I placed her cell phone on the table. "I need you to call Nolan and tell him the deal is on."

"I already told him the deal was off."

"Well, you've had a change of heart," I said.

She lifted a sassy eyebrow. "Do you want to let me out of these handcuffs?"

I pulled my keys from my pocket, walked around the table, and released her wrists.

Sasha rubbed her skin, working out the grooves the cuffs had left behind. She picked up the phone and dialed Nolan. "I changed my mind. Let's do the deal with Viktor."

Nolan sighed. "I just told him I needed more time. He got frustrated and said he was going to go elsewhere."

"Where else is he going to go?" Sasha asked.

"I wish you would have called me earlier. Where have you been? I've been trying to get in touch with you for the last few hours."

"I got sidetracked."

"This is important. I need you to take it seriously."

"Nobody is taking this more seriously than me. I can assure you of that. Call Viktor back and set up a deal. Tell him I've got other buyers waiting to take this off my hands, but I want to do business with him because I want to build a long-term relationship. I think it could be mutually beneficial for the two of us. And he's not going to find this quality anywhere else."

An exasperated sigh escaped Nolan's mouth again. "I'll see what I can do."

Sasha ended the call.

With more than a little venom in her voice, Foster said, "Just so we're clear. No Viktor, no deal. And you go to jail for 20 years."

52

"She's a flight risk," Foster said as we reconvened in the hallway.

"Where is she going to go?" I asked.

"The Bahamas, Cuba, Mexico. I don't want to have to track her all over hell's half acre."

"You can't keep her in custody. Somebody will put two and two together. She needs to get back to her normal life as soon as possible, working her regular job and doing her regular activities. You can keep a surveillance team on her 24/7."

"I don't have the manpower to do that," Foster said.

"What do you want to do? Put an ankle bracelet on her?"

She considered it for a moment. "That's not such a bad idea."

"And what if somebody sees the bracelet?"

"She got popped on a DUI, and it's part of her probation."

"I think it would raise questions."

"What do you suggest?"

"How about you keep her under surveillance?" Foster suggested.

"Oh, no. We've got other cases."

"So do I." Foster thought about it for a moment. "You've got a prior relationship with her. She can stay with you. It wouldn't raise suspicion."

I lifted a surprised brow. "Absolutely not."

"Why not?"

"You are the one who brought up the whole conflict of interest thing."

"Our case isn't against her anymore. It will be against Viktor Nevsky when Sasha comes through. Just don't sleep with her again."

I looked at the sheriff.

"I'm staying out of this one."

"I've got a simpler solution," JD said. "We get a warrant and put tracking software on her phone. She won't even know about it. We'll know where she is at all times. If she tries to run, it will be easy to find her. Or we can just have Isabella do it."

Foster considered it for a moment. "Fine. Let's go with that."

"I'll work on the warrant," Daniels said.

I wanted to put things in motion. I called Isabella and asked her to send spyware to Sasha's phone. I still had it with me. Isabella sent a text message. Then I clicked the link and downloaded the app. It would run continuously in the background. Once it was installed, I deleted the text from Isabella. Sasha would be none the wiser. The app would monitor all calls and record them, as well as track her location. It would send the files to a remote server.

When Sasha was released, I gave her back her personal effects, then JD and I took her back to her apartment.

Sasha didn't say a word to me until we pulled into the parking lot. "I assume you have me under surveillance?"

"Nope."

"That's mighty trusting of you."

"I have faith that you will come through."

"Is my phone tapped?"

"You're on the honor system," I said, not divulging any additional details. It wasn't an outright lie—more like an omission. I hated that we were in this situation.

She scoffed. "Why do I find that hard to believe?"

"You've been handed the golden ticket. I suggest you take this opportunity and play by the rules," I said. "Do everything you're supposed to do, and you walk away from this like it never happened."

"No scars, huh?"

"Something like that," I said. "Here are the rules. You're going to stay in your apartment, and you're not going to leave except for work or food. Anytime you leave, you send me a text and tell me where you're going and for how long."

"That's kinda stalker-ish."

"Be glad you don't have an ankle bracelet."

She frowned at me. "So, I'm basically grounded."

"You'll live," I said. "Do what you're supposed to, and this will be all over in no time. You'll have your life back."

She gave me that skeptical look again.

"Let me know the minute you hear back from Nolan."

I climbed out of the Porsche, pulled the seat forward, and held the door for her.

She climbed out of the car. "Relax. I'm not going to do anything to screw this up. But what happens if Viktor figures out this is a setup?"

"If you keep your mouth shut and keep up the act, he's never gonna know."

She gave me a doubtful look. "How did you figure this all out, anyway?"

I shrugged.

Her eyes narrowed, trying to read my mind. She wasn't successful. Sasha gave up and strutted into the lobby of her apartment building.

I climbed back into the Porsche.

JD said, "You think she's gonna run?"

"She'd be a fool to pass up this deal."

JD pulled out of the parking lot, and we headed to Coconut General to speak with Mike. We caught up with him in the trauma unit. He had pins in his leg, holding everything together. Part of the bone had shattered during his fall. He wasn't going anywhere anytime soon.

Mike didn't look exceptionally pleased to see us, either. His face twisted with a scowl. "What do you want?"

I forced a smile. "How are you feeling?"

"How do you think I'm feeling?"

"We just have a few questions for you."

"Why would I talk to you?"

"Because Vernon fingered you as one of the kidnappers."

"Vernon doesn't know what he had for breakfast yesterday. It's not going to hold up."

It was an area of concern.

"I'm not so sure about that," I said. "This whole adventure seems to have opened up areas of Vernon's brain that were previously closed off. He remembers all kinds of things."

Mike stiffened and swallowed hard.

"So, tell me how this whole thing went down," I said.

"What's in it for me?"

"There's still one, possibly two, kidnappers at large. Work with the prosecution, and maybe you will get a reduced sentence. Right now, you're looking at life."

His skin was pale. Kidnapping was akin to murder as far as punishment went in Florida.

"Besides," I continued. "Otis killed your girlfriend. Don't you want a little payback?"

53

M ike's jaw tightened, and his eyes brimmed. "I'm not saying anything without a lawyer."

He didn't specifically ask for a lawyer, so technically, the conversation wasn't over.

"Here's what I think happened," I said. "You tell me if I'm right or wrong."

He said nothing.

"I think Vernon told one of you his wild tales about war bonds. I think you told Otis. I think Otis came up with the idea to kidnap Vernon. Then I think you and Monica double-crossed him. You took Vernon out one night, put him up on Monica's boat, and planned to get the war bonds yourself, cutting Otis out of the deal. But Otis didn't like that too much. So, he took Vernon from Monica. He had to kill her because she would recognize him, even though he was wearing a mask. He would have killed you too if you'd been around."

Judging by the recognition in Mike's eyes, I knew I was right on target.

My words soaked in for a few moments.

"Otis isn't working alone," I said. "He's got an accomplice. Do you have any idea who that might be?"

Mike finally admitted, "He's tight with a guy named Gage. We all had a few beers together one time."

"Were you friends with Otis?"

"I guess at one point in time. I mean, it's not like we were really close or anything. But as coworkers, we had a good relationship," he said.

"I'll need you to testify against him."

"Give me a deal, and we'll talk. The whole thing was his idea. We'd have never done it if he didn't put that bug in our ear," he said, trying to shift blame.

I don't think he realized what he admitted to.

I videotaped the statement, then returned to the station and filled out an application for a warrant for Otis.

We didn't have any corroborating evidence, and Mike's testimony was suspect at best. But Echols signed off on the warrant. JD and I put together a small tactical team and headed over to Sunset Palms. We stormed the main entrance, trying not to alarm the residents.

I greeted the receptionist at the front desk with a smile and asked for Otis.

Her nervous eyes flicked between all of us. It wasn't every day that law enforcement officers, decked out in tactical gear, shouldering AR-15s, showed up at the assisted living facility.

"I can ask him to come to the front desk, if you like," she said.

"That would be perfect," I replied.

Her voice crackled over the intercom, echoing throughout the facility.

A few minutes later, Otis lumbered around the corner and stepped toward the front desk. His eyes rounded when he saw us. He spun around and took off down the hallway in the direction that he came.

I chased after him.

A few elderly individuals navigated the hallway, one with the assistance of a walker, another helped along by a cane. I was concerned he'd knock one of them over. Their frail bodies wouldn't survive the fall.

Otis blew past them, and thankfully, both residents remained upright. The old man yelled down the hallway after him, "Slow down, you fuck head!"

I slowed up as I passed both of them, then resumed my sprint.

Otis barreled down the hallway and burst through the glass double doors at the end.

I followed him outside, and the tac team charged behind me.

Otis took off across the lot and then bolted up the sidewalk on Centennial Street. He was pretty fast for a big guy.

I sprinted with long strides after him, my chest heaving for breath.

Otis barreled down the sidewalk under the shade of live oaks, passing by trash cans and chain-link fences that surrounded neighboring properties. At the stop sign, he took a sharp right and darted along the lush green hedgerows and under the tall palms of Ocean Mist Boulevard. Cars parked at the curb, lining the narrow roadway.

I was gaining on Otis, and his lack of physical conditioning was starting to take its toll.

I caught up and tackled him to the ground.

He hit the concrete with a groan, and I crashed on top of him.

Otis managed to buck me off, and he sprang to his feet. He came up with a knife and slashed at me as I stood up.

Bad move.

The blade of the small tactical knife glimmered in the Florida sunshine. The blade whooshed inches from my face.

POP!

POP!

Erickson had shouldered his rifle and fired two shots at the perp, knocking him to the ground before he could draw my blood.

A geyser of crimson erupted from Otis's chest and one from his throat. He clutched his wound as blood spurted from his carotid artery onto the sidewalk. His eyes went round as he gasped and gurgled for breath.

I kicked the knife away, knelt down, and applied pressure to the wound.

Within a few moments, Otis stopped twitching and convulsing.

With my hands soaked in blood, I backed away, grimacing at the scene.

JD called dispatch.

"He could have killed you," Erickson said as he caught up to me, his eyes surveying his handiwork.

"I didn't know you cared," I snarked.

"You'd have done the same for me," he said.

"Yeah, but now we have no link to his accomplice."

Erickson just shook his head. "Ungrateful."

It was a justified shooting. Still, I would have liked to have gotten information from Otis about his partner in crime. There was no way he pulled this off alone.

First responders swarmed. EMTs and paramedics made an effort to bring Otis back. But the writing was on the wall.

Paris Delaney and her crew had arrived in time to soak up the gory footage. Dietrich snapped photos, and forensic investigators chronicled the scene. Brenda examined the remains.

Erickson would be put on administrative leave pending the outcome of an investigation.

Brenda and her crew bagged the body, and the remains were loaded into the back of the medical examiner's van.

Paris closed in with her camera crew. "What can you tell us about the shooting?"

"No comment at this time," I said.

I wasn't about to say anything under these circumstances.

We left the scene, headed back to the station, and filled out after-action reports. By that time, JD and I were ready to find a happy hour somewhere.

We left the station and headed up to Oyster Avenue. But instead of having a relaxing drink, JD wanted to go to Flanagan's to look for trouble.

"I don't think this is such a good idea," I said as he found a place to park on the side street.

He looked at me like I was crazy. "Relax. We're just going in for one drink."

"One drink is all it's going to take," I said.

"Don't be scared. I'll protect you."

I sneered at him.

He killed the engine and hopped out of the car. I climbed out and followed him down the block to the Irish pub. I knew there was a method to his madness, but I wasn't sure this was the best way to go about it.

We pushed into the bar and glanced around. I saw a few familiar faces, but Rafferty wasn't here. Neither was Rexford.

Our presence drew a few curious stares from other deputies in plain clothes.

We moved to the bar, took a seat, and ordered a round.

"You going to ask us to leave again?" JD asked the bartender.

He gave Jack a flat look. "What can I get for you?"

"I'll tell you what you can get for me. Rafferty's glass after he finishes his drink."

The bartender's face wrinkled. Then he connected the dots. "What makes you think he's coming in tonight?"

"Doesn't matter when he comes in. Just save his glass next time."

"Look, I don't need any trouble. I just pour the drinks. I don't get involved."

It was at that moment when Rafferty and Rexford pushed into the bar. They were laughing and joking until they saw us. Their eyes threw daggers as they hesitated just inside the doorway. Not to be deterred, they marched forward, muttered a few derisive comments as they passed by, and took a seat at the far end of the bar.

54

"Get them a pitcher of beer and put it on my tab," JD said.

The bartender gave him a hesitant look, then complied. He pulled the tap and filled the pitcher with golden liquid. He delivered the frothy goodness with two frozen mugs. "Compliments of Mr. Donovan."

Both of their faces twisted with revulsion.

"Send it back," Rafferty said. "I can buy my own goddamn beer."

His angry eyes found JD and me, and he flipped us off with enthusiasm, making a snarling face.

JD smiled and waved.

Rafferty and Rexford ordered their drinks and sat at the end of the bar, grumbling and giving us dirty looks.

The bartender returned with the pitcher of beer. "What do you want me to do with this?"

"Give it to somebody," JD said. He looked around the bar and told him to send it to a table of ladies in a booth against the wall.

A waitress delivered the beer and pointed to JD. The ladies smiled and nodded in appreciation, and Jack waved back.

By that time, Rexford had made his way over to us. "You got a lot of nerve to come back here. How about you take your little curious selves somewhere else?"

"What's the matter?" JD said. "Rafferty can't stand up for himself? He's gotta send you over here?"

Rexford's face reddened, and his jaw tensed.

The bartender looked on with unease.

I tried to diffuse the situation. "It's out of our hands. IA is handling it."

"There's nothing to handle," Rexford said. "This is a goddamn witch hunt."

"Why is he hiding behind a lawyer?" JD asked.

"So he doesn't get railroaded by fuckheads like you."

"He could provide a DNA sample and be done with it," JD muttered.

Rexford clenched his teeth. "I hope to God you idiots find yourselves on the wrong side of an accusation. We may just find out you two aren't so squeaky clean. Where does all that money come from, Jack?"

Only JD's close friends called him Jack, and Rexford certainly didn't qualify.

"Let's keep it civil," the bartender said. "Or do I need to ask one of you to leave?"

"We were here first," JD said.

"This ain't none of your business," Rexford said to the bartender. "Just keep your mouth shut and keep pouring drinks."

The bartender didn't like that.

"Run along and sit down," JD said. "You've already made a big enough ass out of yourself."

Steam was about to come out of Rexford's ears. He glared at JD, his cheeks reddening. His hands balled into fists.

I think the bartender was a few moments away from calling the cops. But I'm sure he was a little bit hesitant to call the police on the police.

"I've had enough of your mouth," Rexford said.

"We can step outside, and you can try to shut me up," JD said with a smile.

I climbed off my barstool and stood in between the two. "Let's all just take a deep breath before something happens that everybody regrets."

Rexford and I stared each other down for a moment. I was ready for anything.

He finally took a step back. "You two ought to watch your back."

"Keep talking shit," JD said, egging him on.

Rexford shouted around me. "Keep hiding behind your bodyguard."

JD finished the last swallow of his drink, then climbed off his bar stool. "I'll be outside if you want to settle this."

Jack strutted toward the door, waved to the ladies, and pushed outside.

Rexford fumed.

"Make a smart decision for once," I said. "Go sit down."

By that time, Rafferty had joined the fray. He pulled on Rexford's arm. "Let it go. I can fight my own battles. This is gonna do more harm than good. Besides, I'm innocent. When all this is said and done, that's gonna be abundantly clear. And these two are gonna look like bigger idiots than they already are."

Rafferty coaxed Rexford back to his barstool.

I paid the tab and stepped outside.

JD was pumped and ready to go. "Is he coming?"

I shook my head.

Jack frowned. "I figured he'd wuss out."

I laughed and suggested we hit Oyster Avenue. The last thing either of us needed was to get into a smackdown with those two morons.

The sun had set, and the avenue brimmed with activity as tourists wandered up and down the boulevard. Music from bands spilled into the street, and the air swirled with the aroma of grilled food. Everyone was having a good time. I figured we deserved to have a good time, too.

But the Universe had other plans.

55

"**Y**our girlfriend's on the move," Isabella said when she called.

"She's not my girlfriend," I reiterated.

"Where's she headed?"

"She's headed north on Coral Cove now. I'm not sure where she's going."

"She was supposed to text me if she left her apartment."

"Looks like she's not playing by the rules."

I stayed on the line with Isabella and told JD about the new development. We hustled back to the Porsche, hopped in, and sped across the island. Isabella kept us updated, giving us directions.

We ended up at the Mega Mart.

I scanned the parking lot for Sasha's car but didn't see it anywhere. I asked Isabella, "Are you sure this is the correct location?"

"She's there right now."

The place was open 24 hours a day, but at this time of night there wasn't near as much traffic. There was the usual section of campers and RVs where people would bivouac for the night and sometimes longer. It was sanctioned by the store and created business for them.

My eyes finally locked on the target. I told Isabella I'd call her back.

Viktor Nevsky marched Sasha toward a small box truck. It looked like he had a gun in her rib cage, but he was discreet about it. He was with another goon who was quite a bit larger and kept his head on a swivel. They moved around to the back of the box truck, which was parked at the far end of the lot, along with the other campers and RVs. There was a row of hedges behind it, and some live oaks covered the area.

"What the hell do you think's going on?" JD muttered.

"I think she's taking him to the hundred million in counterfeit bills. Maybe he figured out she was trying to set him up. Or maybe he planned to rip her off all along. Who knows?"

"Helluva place to store it," JD said. "How do you want to play this?"

I called for backup, then we hopped out of the car and approached the box truck. We stayed out of view, huddling close to campers and minivans as we advanced.

The box truck had been backed into the parking space. The front grill faced outward. From our position, the rear of the vehicle was obscured by an RV.

The cargo door rattled as it opened. It sounded like Viktor was inspecting the merchandise.

JD and I held up at the front grill of an RV that was parked next to the box truck. I angled my pistol around the vehicle and took aim at Nevsky's goon, who was standing just to the side of the vehicle.

"Freeze!" I shouted. "Coconut County."

The goon darted behind the box truck, taking cover.

The parking lot was not the ideal place to get into a gunfight. There were too many people around. No place is particularly ideal to get into a gunfight, but some are worse than others.

Viktor's goon let us know exactly what he thought of law enforcement. He angled his pistol around the back of the truck and opened fire.

Muzzle flash flickered from the barrel, and bullets snapped past my ear, racing across the parking lot.

I ducked for cover behind the front grill of the RV, and JD huddled beside me.

Nevsky and his goon hustled around the far side of the box truck and climbed in through the passenger door. The goon slid behind the wheel and cranked up the engine.

Nevsky had forced Sasha into the vehicle in between them. I dared not take a shot at the goon. I didn't want to put a stray bullet in Sasha.

Nevsky's goon put the box truck into gear and stomped the pedal. The diesel rumbled, and brown exhaust spewed.

I took the opportunity to shoot out the left rear tire of the box truck. It had dual rear wheels on either side, so blowing out one tire did little to hinder its forward progression. The rubber screeched against the asphalt as the truck barreled out of the parking space and headed across the lot toward the nearest exit.

JD had already started running back to the Porsche. He hopped in, cranked up the engine, and pulled alongside me. I climbed inside, pulled the door shut, and buckled my safety harness.

I knew we were in for a wild ride.

I called dispatch and updated them on the situation and told them to get Tango One in the air.

The box truck wouldn't be able to outrun us, that was for certain. But it had advantages. It was built like a tank. It rolled out of the parking lot and took a left on Inverness Lane.

We were right on its tail.

Distant sirens drew near.

The box truck barreled ahead to the next intersection.

A car was stopped in the right lane, but that didn't deter the goon. He just smashed into the back of it, pushed the vehicle into the intersection, where it was hit by cross traffic and spun around.

Metal crumpled and crinkled, and shards of glass and plastic scattered.

Tires squealed. The box truck navigated around the mess

and continued through the intersection as horns honked. More tires squealed, attempting to avoid collision.

JD pulled to the intersection, and I hopped out to check on the driver of the car the box truck had pushed into the intersection. She was just climbing out of her car.

"Are you okay?" I asked.

She looked dazed and disoriented. "Yeah. I think so."

"EMTs are on the way."

She nodded.

The guy that had T-boned her stepped out of his Super Duty. He moved around to the front of his truck. It was battered and bruised, but hadn't suffered near the amount of damage.

He didn't seem any worse for the wear.

I hopped back into the Porsche. The light had turned green for us, but traffic was backed up in all directions. JD stomped on the gas, and the engine howled as he navigated around the wreckage.

The box truck was a few hundred yards down the street by this point.

We sailed down the avenue, hitting the triple digits.

The box truck took a left on Ocean Whisper, and JD followed.

The goons hadn't managed to get the cargo door shut all the way, and with each bump, it bounced up higher, revealing more of the cargo within.

There was a pallet that had been secured with a tarp and bungee cord. I couldn't say for certain what was underneath the tarp, but I had a pretty good idea.

56

The box truck banked a hard right on Paradise Park.

We were right behind it.

The pallet slid to the left side of the cargo area. One of the bungee straps had come undone, and the tarp flapped with the breeze.

The truck barreled down the narrow residential street. Cars were parked on either side. It blazed through a few stop signs, but at this time of night, there wasn't much traffic in the area.

This was probably one of the slower-speed chases we had been involved in. They weren't going to get away.

The box truck took another hard left, and the pallet slid to the right side of the truck.

JD and I followed as the truck motored up to another major intersection.

The goon laid on the horn, and the box truck hung a hard right. The momentum of the truck tipped it up on its left side, and the remaining left rear tire blew out from the added stress.

Rubber peeled from the rim, flapped around underneath the truck, then scattered into the roadway.

Sparks showered from the rim as it ground against concrete.

It was a miracle the box truck didn't tip over.

The truck clipped a stalled car in the right lane that had hazards flashing. The truck's right tire, already elevated, ran over the back bumper of the small import. It was like a monster truck show as it rolled over the back of the vehicle, collapsing the rear end. It was enough to topple the already teetering truck.

The box truck crashed onto its side and skidded across the road. The pallet of money flew out the back of the truck. The tarp came free, and stacks of counterfeit money scattered.

The traffic behind came to a stop.

It didn't take long for people to see the money in the street. People stopped their cars, hopped out, and gathered all they could.

Like sharks to blood, people swarmed.

JD pulled over, and I hopped out of the car, drew my weapon, and advanced toward the box truck.

The right rear tire still spun.

The smell of gasoline and oil permeated the air.

Viktor Nevsky pushed open the passenger side door, which was now facing skyward. He climbed out of the truck, pistol in hand. His eyes scanned the surroundings and saw me approaching.

He took aim and blasted off a few shots.

Muzzle flash flickered, and bullets streaked through the night air.

I kept moving, took aim, and squeezed the trigger twice.

The pistol hammered against my palm, and the bullets found their target.

Blood spewed from Victor's neck and head.

He tumbled back, fell into the cab, and the door closed on top of him.

Sasha's screams filtered out of the cab. She had a dead, bloody guy on top of her.

The feeding frenzy in the street continued. Traffic was backed up in both directions. A sea of headlights and taillights.

I advanced to the truck, climbed up onto the side of the cab, and cautiously pulled the door open.

Sasha had managed to slip around the dead guy. She climbed out of the cab, covered in speckles of Viktor's blood.

I kept my weapon aimed inside at the goon behind the wheel, but the crash had knocked him out cold. His head had smashed the side of the window.

JD joined me, and we pulled Viktor's body out of the truck and let him fall to the street. By that time, the goon was coming around. He moaned and groaned and tried to get his bearings.

With my weapon aimed at him, I shouted, "Coconut County. You're under arrest."

He thought about reaching for the pistol in his waistband for a second, then decided better of it. He kept his hands in the air, and I told him to get out of the vehicle.

He climbed out slowly as we kept our weapons aimed at him. As soon as he was out of the truck, I slammed him to the ground and slapped cuffs around his wrists, then took his pistol and tossed it aside.

The patter of rotor blades circled overhead, and Tango One spotlit the scene with an otherworldly blue beam.

The money in the street had caused a scene of pure chaos as people fought over cash.

With the threat neutralized, I moved to the pile of money, displayed my badge, and shouted at the hoard to back off.

Nobody paid any attention.

They kept grabbing handfuls of money.

I shouted again, and a few of them took off running while others continued to scoop up handfuls. It was almost all gone by this point. The crowd had devoured the stash in no time.

I managed to run off the rest of the money grabbers. There were only a few stacks of the counterfeit bills left.

Patrol units arrived, and first responders flooded the scene.

Paris and her crew arrived.

I made my way back to Sasha. "Are you okay?"

She nodded. "I guess you got the bad guy. Does that mean I'm off the hook?"

"You weren't supposed to leave your apartment without contacting me."

She gave me a flat look. "He kidnapped me. That gives me a pass."

"You should have the EMTs check you out."

"I'm fine," she assured.

Agent Foster made it to the scene, and I filled her in on the situation. She wasn't thrilled about all that money getting into circulation. But she'd have to take the good with the bad. Viktor Nevsky was no longer breathing. Though I think she would have preferred to be the one to shoot him.

We wrapped up at the scene, and I was put on administrative leave pending the outcome of an investigation. It was standard procedure. I surrendered my duty weapon and filled out a report.

After we finished up at the station, JD and I took Agent Foster out for a celebratory drink. We filled her in on all the events that led up to the chase. It was the first time I'd seen Foster smile since I met her.

"I've gotta hand it to you. I didn't have a lot of faith in you guys, but you came through."

"We aim to please," JD said.

"So what happens to Sasha?"

Foster shrugged. "She lived up to her end of the deal. Now she just needs to walk us through her process and flip on all her suppliers and co-conspirators." She paused. "You're not thinking there's a future between you two, are you?"

I laughed and shook my head.

"Good. I was going to have to wonder about you."

"Trust me, I don't think that's even an option. We're barely on speaking terms."

We drank good whiskey, told stories, and chilled out for the rest of the evening. It was around last call when my phone buzzed. I didn't think the sheriff would be calling at this hour, especially since I was on leave. I pulled the phone from my pocket and looked at the screen. The number came from the hospital. I swiped the screen and took the call.

Lamonte's voice filtered through the speaker. "I just remembered who shot me."

Ready for more?

The adventure continues with Wild Grave!

Join my newsletter and find out what happens next!

AUTHOR'S NOTE

Thanks for taking this incredible journey with me. I'm having such a blast writing about Tyson and JD, and I've got plenty more adventures to come. I hope you'll stick around for the wild ride.

Thanks for all the great reviews and kind words!

If you liked this book, let me know with a review on Amazon.

Thanks for reading!

—*Tripp*

TYSON WILD

Wild Ocean

Wild Justice

Wild Rivera

Wild Tide

Wild Rain

Wild Captive

Wild Killer

Wild Honor

Wild Gold

Wild Case

Wild Crown

Wild Break

Wild Fury

Wild Surge

Wild Impact

Wild L.A.

Wild High

Wild Abyss

Wild Life

Wild Spirit

Wild Thunder

Wild Season

Wild Rage

Wild Heart

Wild Spring

Wild Outlaw

Wild Revenge

Wild Secret

Wild Envy

Wild Surf

Wild Venom

Wild Island

Wild Demon

Wild Blue

Wild Lights

Wild Target

Wild Jewel

Wild Greed

Wild Sky

Wild Storm

Wild Bay

Wild Chaos

Wild Cruise

Wild Catch

Wild Encounter

Wild Blood

Wild Vice

Wild Winter

Wild Malice

Wild Fire

Wild Deceit

Wild Massacre

Wild Illusion

Wild Mermaid

Wild Star

Wild Skin

Wild Prodigy

Wild Sport

Wild Hex

Wild West

Wild Alpine

Wild Execution

Wild Tomb

Wild Immortal

Wild Widow

Wild Impulse

Wild Moon

Wild Rocket

Wild Dynasty

Wild Luck

Wild Hero

Wild Grave

Wild...

CONNECT WITH ME

I'm just a geek who loves to write. Follow me on Facebook.

www.trippellis.com

Made in the USA
Columbia, SC
10 October 2024

44097033R00178